The Epic of Gilgamesh

The Epic of
GILGAMESH

Translated, with an Introduction, by

MAUREEN GALLERY KOVACS

Stanford University Press
Stanford, California

Stanford University Press
Stanford, California

© 1985, 1989 by the Board of Trustees of the
Leland Stanford Junior University
Printed in the United States of America

Stanford University Press publications are distributed
exclusively by Stanford University Press within the
United States, Canada, Mexico, and Central America;
they are distributed exclusively by Cambridge University
Press throughout the rest of the world.

Original printing 1989
Last figure below indicates year of this printing:
04   03   02   01   00   99   98   97   96   95

Library of Congress Cataloging-in-Publication Data

Gilgamesh. English.
  The epic of Gilgamesh / translated with an introduction by
Maureen Gallery Kovacs.
    p.   cm.
  Translation of: Gilgamesh.
  ISBN 0-8047-1589-0 (alk. paper):   ISBN 0-8047-1711-7
(pbk.)
  I. Kovacs, Maureen Gallery.   II. Title.
PJ377I.G5E5   1989
892' .I —dc19   89-4318
                                                      CIP

To my husband, Frank

ACKNOWLEDGMENTS

This new translation of the Epic of Gilgamesh is a much revised version of one initially undertaken at the request of Professors Ted Good and Curtis Runnels for a course at Stanford University. I had long thought of doing one, and had over the years assembled the source documents and secondary commentary which are scattered in many publications. Their enthusiasm and need for a new English translation provided the incentive finally to tackle the project. The scholarly studies on the Epic are numerous indeed, and I was not far into this research before I "remembered" why I had not done it earlier, but by then it was too late to back out. I also made an unexpected discovery, that making a good translation for the general reader is more difficult than making one for the specialist, where one can alternately defend or excuse one's translation in an infinite series of learned footnotes.

When the Humanities Editor at Stanford University Press, Helen Tartar, proposed publishing the translation along with some introductory and explanatory material, she could not have anticipated the number of rewrites that were to come. First, the original translation required a thorough revision and updating in view of newly published articles. Further, while the ancient tablets dictate the essence of the translated text, the scope of the introduction was a subjective decision, involving dreaded compromise between comprehensiveness and comprehensibility. I can only praise Helen's wisdom in assigning as editor Peter J. Kahn, who helped me—kindly but very firmly—to refine a mass of academic detail to an intelligible and appropriate level.

The handsome map on p. xxxvi is the work of Thomas A. Drain of San Francisco.

Lastly, I must acknowledge the sacrifice of my husband Frank, who saw deadlines for resuming normal life come and go. I apologize too for ruining a beautiful piece of literature for him, for he has "lived with Gilgamesh" too long to ever actually want to read the translation.

M. G. K.

CONTENTS

The Epic of
GILGAMESH

A NOTE TO THE READER

I have kept references to the scholarly literature to a minimum in the footnotes, and books and articles mentioned are cited in full when they occur. Two books and two articles come up so regularly, though, that it seemed best to give full citations for them here and only short forms in the notes. Below I list first the forms the reader will encounter in the notes and then the full citations for these four works:

Collon, *First Impressions*

Dominique Collon, *First Impressions* (Chicago: Univ. of Chicago Press, 1988).

Foster, "Gilgamesh: Sex, Love and the Ascent of Knowledge"

Benjamin R. Foster, "Gilgamesh: Sex, Love and the Ascent of Knowledge," in John H. Marks and Robert M. Good, eds., *Love & Death in the Ancient Near East* (Guilford, Conn.: Four Quarters Publishing Co., 1987), pp. 21–42.

Lambert, "Gilgamesh in Literature and Art"

W. G. Lambert, "Gilgamesh in Literature and Art: The Second and First Millennia," in Ann Farkas et al., *Monsters and Demons in the Ancient and Medieval Worlds* (Mainz: Verlag Philipp von Zabern, 1987), pp. 37–52.

Tigay, *Evolution*

Jeffrey H. Tigay, *The Evolution of the Gilgamesh Epic* (Philadelphia: Univ. of Penn. Press, 1982).

A NOTE ON THE
TRANSLATION

The present translation of the Standard Version of the Epic of Gilgamesh is based on the tablets and articles published through the fall of 1988.* All translation is interpretation to some degree, reflecting the translator's style, sensitivity, and approach; I have tried to keep to a somewhat literal rendering of the Akkadian words, grammar, and images, without attempting to recast the poetry of the Akkadian into English poetry. Most of the differences between this and older translations are not stylistic in any event, but result from the major advances in the recovery of the tablets, the reconstruction of the text from fragments, the discovery of helpful parallels, and our knowledge of the language. In relatively few instances is the reading or meaning of a word still in dispute; when alternatives are important they are indicated in parentheses.

The reader will no doubt find that some lines seem totally obscure. In general, this will be an accurate reflection of the original. The reasons for such obscurity might be the incomplete preservation of the lines, a scribal misunderstanding of the meaning of the original that he was copying, or damage resulting in confusion in later copies. Some passages that are relatively clear and consistent in the Old Babylonian version, for example, are obscure and awkward in the Standard Version.

The reader may encounter difficulties with the frequent mentions of gods and places. I have provided a Glossary of all proper names mentioned in the text, but to annotate all the linguistic, historical, and literary associations would only distract the general reader from the central points of the story. Occasional footnotes do provide additional information on essential, unusual or disputed points.

* There is so far no up-to-date edition of all the original tablets of the Epic of Gilgamesh. The tablets from Nineveh and Babylon, now in the British Museum, which provide the bulk of the text, are published as a composite in R. Campbell Thompson, *The Epic of Gilgamish* (Oxford: Clarendon Press, 1930), but many other fragments discovered since then are scattered in various Assyriological books and journals. A complete re-edition of the text is being prepared by W. G. Lambert, Irving Finkel, and Andrew George, and will become the new standard reference.

A few words are in order about the treatment of variants. This translation represents a composite of all the Standard Version tablets. When there is no Standard Version text preserved, I have had recourse to the Old Babylonian version to provide continuity of narrative. In a few particularly interesting cases (e.g., in Tablets II and X), I have commented on and cited Old Babylonian variants in footnotes, but always in such a way as not to break the flow of the story. Missing words are occasionally supplied from other versions, without comment. The existence of variants, either from other tablets of the Standard Version or from earlier versions (e.g., Old Babylonian parallels to Standard Version passages), is generally not noted.

A missing word or line is indicated by three ellipsis points (. . .). Where a section or entire passage is lost, I have indicated the approximate number of lines in square brackets. In many instances, however, the missing words, lines, or even passages can be restored on the basis of parallels from another part of the tablet, another tablet of the same version, or even another version, because verbatim repetition is a hallmark of Mesopotamian literature. Such restoration is particularly heavy in Tablets IV and X. Because the Epic of Gilgamesh draws heavily on other literary works, they too can be used to restore damaged parts of the Epic. For example, parts of the Flood Story in Tablet XI are restored from the Myth of Atrahasis. Restorations that I judge are fairly certain, such as those based on parallel passages, are not indicated at all. In some cases missing words have been supplied by the obvious demands of context or by conjecture; these are in italics. If a restoration is more uncertain, a question mark in parentheses follows the word or phrase. The occasional word added by the translator to clarify the sense of a passage is enclosed in parentheses. This system suffers from some ambiguity, but to add more technical typographical conventions would make reading very tedious.

Gaps in the physical text are not the only source of uncertainty. Sometimes a word is perfectly preserved but its meaning is unknown, at least in the present context. If a translation is ventured here, it too is followed by a question mark; otherwise the word is left in Akkadian.

As an aid to the reader in following this long text, I have supplied descriptive section headings and distinguished narrative from direct speech by indenting the latter as well as using quotation marks. The tablets themselves contain no headings, and indeed, cuneiform has no special symbols to indicate paragraphs, direct speech, questions, exclamations, or emphasis. The only visual indication of subdivision or structure within a tablet is the occasional incised line drawn across a column to indicate a change of speaker or episode, but even such lines are not consistently present. Furthermore, different copies of the same passage will not always have dividing lines in the same places, so their structural significance should not be overestimated.

Translators normally number lines by indicating the column and line number of the cuneiform tablet as published, for ease of checking the translation against the cuneiform. Since this translation will be used by the general reader, I feel that consecutive line numbers for this composite text are more useful. In some poorly preserved tablets the line numbering following a large break is merely a guess. Though I have generally followed the line divisions of the standard publications, I have divided or joined some lines for visual balance. It is worth noting that the distribution of text across the tablets' surface varies considerably from tablet to tablet, even in the case of tablets found at the same site.

INTRODUCTION

The Epic of Gilgamesh recounts the deeds of a famous hero-king of ancient Mesopotamia and is rich with adventure and encounters with strange creatures, men and gods alike. But though these provide a lively and exotic story line, the central concerns of the Epic are really human relationships and feelings—loneliness, friendship, love, loss, revenge, regret, and the fear of the oblivion of death. These themes are developed in a distinctly Mesopotamian idiom, to be sure, but with a sensitivity and intensity that touch the modern reader across the chasm of three thousand years.

In spite of its direct appeal to modern sensibilities, the Epic is little read outside of academic circles because it is thought to be obscure and difficult to understand. True, the text of the Epic is still physically incomplete, breaking the continuity of the story, and the meaning of some words is not known. But the Epic is currently far more complete and understandable than the existing translations in English suggest. Over the last twenty years much progress has been made in recovering the text—newly found pieces have filled in gaps in the text, and the meanings of many words are better understood. But though revised translations have appeared in many other languages, translations into English have not kept in step. The present translation is intended to make the Epic of Gilgamesh accessible to the English-speaking general reader in as complete and readable a form as possible.

The existence of the Epic has been known to the modern world for only the last 120 years, since shortly after the decipherment of cuneiform writing. The Epic was written in the dialect of the Akkadian language reserved for written literature called Standard Babylonian. In its complete state the Epic comprises about 2,900 lines written on eleven clay tablets.* The tablets so far recovered represent some eight to twelve copies of the Epic, most found in the palace and temple libraries at Nineveh ("King Ashurbanipal's library") in Assyria, and dating to the seventh century B.C. Other tablets have been found in the northern Mesopotamian sites of Assur, Nimrud, and Sultantepe, and in the southern Mesopotamian sites of Uruk (the ancestral city of Gilgamesh)

---

* Different copies of the Epic distribute the text on the tablets in different ways, so the notion of a "line" has no literary significance, nor is the count precise.

FIGURE 1. A fragmentary tablet containing text from the eleventh tablet of
the Epic of Gilgamesh, illustrating the condition of the text even after many
pieces have been rejoined. Tablet K.8517, reproduced by courtesy of the Trust-
ees of the British Museum.

and Babylon. Though hardened clay is more resistant to decay by time
and the elements than other substances, many tablets have been se-
verely damaged and are in fragmentary condition. (See Figure 1.) Con-
sequently, only some 60 percent of the text of the Epic is now pre-
served, though some missing parts can be restored on the basis of
parallel passages. Recent archaeological discoveries offer good reason
to expect that the complete text of the Epic will be known within this
generation. In 1986 the Iraqi archaeologists excavating at Sippar (cen-
tral Iraq) discovered an intact library dating to about the late sixth
century B.C. containing complete literary tablets still on their shelves.

A complete "Myth of Atrahasis" (Flood Story) has been reported, and there is a real possibility that a complete Gilgamesh Epic will also be identified.

Brief Summary of the Epic

The first tablet opens with a narrator praising the wisdom of Gilgamesh, a famous king of old who left eternal monuments of both his royal and personal accomplishments.* According to the narrator, the Epic of Gilgamesh was written by Gilgamesh himself, and the very tablet (or stela) on which he wrote his experiences was deposited in the foundation of the city wall of Uruk, where it remains available for all to read. Gilgamesh is described as two-thirds divine and one-third human, extraordinary in strength and beauty. However, he oppresses the young men and women of Uruk in some way, and the gods respond by creating a counterpart to him. In sharp contrast to Gilgamesh, Enkidu is a primal man, born and raised in the wilderness with the wild beasts, who sets free the animals caught by trappers. These super- and sub-human counterparts are brought together in a classic confrontation of civilization against nature, as a trapper uses a harlot from Uruk to deplete Enkidu of his animal powers. Abandoned by the wild beasts, Enkidu then adopts the ways of civilized men and eventually goes to Uruk to meet and challenge Gilgamesh. After a wrestling match in which Gilgamesh prevails, Enkidu acknowledges Gilgamesh as the legitimate superior and they become devoted friends, the first time either has felt true companionship. After some time, however, Enkidu's natural forces soften with city life and Gilgamesh proposes a dangerous adventure to the Cedar Forest. There they will slay the Guardian, Humbaba the Terrible, and cut down the sacred Cedar and achieve eternal fame. Despite strong protests from his citizen advisers and the tearful pleadings of his mother, Gilgamesh sets off with Enkidu, taking special weapons and relying on the promised protection of the Sun God. During the six-day journey Gilgamesh has terrifying and ominous dreams, but they go on. Once they reach the Cedar Forest, however, Enkidu wants to turn back, realizing the gravity of what they are about to do. The Sun God urges them to go in, and they confront Humbaba. The interchanges with Humbaba are, unfortunately, fragmentary and difficult to understand, but eventually Enkidu persuades Gilgamesh to kill

---

* A fuller summary of the events of each tablet is given before the tablet in the translation.

him. While they are cutting down cedars, Enkidu proposes making of the tallest one a door for the temple of the chief god in order to placate him. Back in Uruk, the hero Gilgamesh is approached by the beautiful goddess Ishtar, who wants him to marry her. Knowing the fate of her other lovers, he rejects her violently and incurs her enmity. She sends the Bull of Heaven down to wreak havoc in the city, but the two friends manage to slay it. The gods, faced with the heroes' double offense of killing the Guardian of the Cedar Forest and the Bull of Heaven, decide that one of the two must die, and that it must be Enkidu. He suffers a long and painful death, attended to the last by his beloved Gilgamesh, who watches by his deathbed and pours out a torrent of memories about their experiences. Gilgamesh is devastated by the loss of his friend and has a statue built in his memory, but the achievement of human fame has now become meaningless in the face of the horror of bodily decay. As a result, Gilgamesh rebels against mortality and sets out to find the secret of eternal life from the only man known to have attained it, the survivor of the Flood, Utanapishtim. Along the treacherous journey he meets with strange and wondrous creatures who all warn him of the impossibility of his quest. His determination to escape his friend's fate drives him on until he finds Utanapishtim's ferryman, who will take him across the Waters of Death. When he finally meets Utanapishtim, Gilgamesh demands to know how he achieved eternal life. Utanapishtim then recites a version of the Flood Story (borrowed from another Mesopotamian myth) and explains that he (with his family and animals) was spared because of his obedience to his personal god, and that they were given eternal life because of his piety. Gilgamesh fails a test of his potential for immortality (to go without sleep) and is sent away. Utanapishtim's wife urges him to give Gilgamesh a consolation gift so he does not have to return to his city empty-handed; Utanapishtim recalls him and reveals a "plant of rejuvenation" that will enable him to live his life over again with the benefit of his new knowledge. Gilgamesh loses the plant to a snake, however, and must return home older and empty-handed after all, for there are no second chances in real life. The story of Gilgamesh's quest ends suddenly where it began, echoing the words of Tablet I which marvel at his extraordinary achievements.

At one level the text indicates that Gilgamesh finds a kind of immortality after all, but only the relative immortality earned by a physical creation—the wall of Uruk—that will outlast him. One should not deduce from this that for the Mesopotamians transcendence over death was available only to those involved in monolithic public works. For at another level one is to understand that Gilgamesh's self-knowledge, as expressed in his tablet of the epic deposited in the foundation of that wall, is what really remains. The final lines consciously hark back to the beginning of the Epic, a paean in praise of Gilgamesh's wisdom and understanding of life.*

The Versions of the Epic

So far I have spoken of "the" Epic of Gilgamesh. It is now time to explain that there exist, in fact, three rather different versions of the Epic of Gilgamesh, composed over a period of nearly 1,000 years. The eleven-tablet[†] version translated here is the best preserved, and is based on the tablets of the first millennium B.C. (Neo-Assyrian period from Assur, Nineveh, Nimrud, and Sultantepe, and Neo- and Late Babylonian periods, from Babylon and Uruk). We have adopted the designation Standard Version because the content and wording seem to have become fairly consistent over a wide area over many centuries.[‡] Later Mesopotamian tradition attributed the authorship of the Epic to a specific individual, Sinleqqiunninni, a scholar-priest of Uruk, possibly dating to the thirteenth century B.C.

As was traditional in Mesopotamian literature, "authorship" consisted largely in the creative adaptation of existing themes and plots

* Foster, "Gilgamesh: Sex, Love and the Ascent of Knowledge." Curiously, the traditional means of ensuring one's memory on earth—establishing a household and having descendants—is completely overlooked in the Epic. Gilgamesh's wife and family are, in fact, conspicuous by their absence. The ancient author certainly knew from other historical documents that Gilgamesh *did* have a son, named Urlugal, who succeeded him as king, and other Gilgamesh material probably known to the author (Siduri's speech in the Old Babylonian version of Tablet X) does allude to Gilgamesh's wife and child, and to establishing a family as the normal "task of *mankind*." A. Leo Oppenheim has used these absences to construct an interpretation of the Epic as a courtly composition for a king who had no son and heir. At the court of such a king, "the topic would be taboo, and the artistry of the court poet strives to treat with delicacy the story of Gilgamesh in order to mirror the tragic fate of his king." Oppenheim, *Ancient Mesopotamia* (2d ed.; Chicago, 1977), pp. 255–63.

† Technically, the Epic of Gilgamesh as known from the Nineveh libraries consists of twelve tablets, but the twelfth shows much evidence of being a secondary addition onto an original eleven-tablet series, as explained in Appendix B. Therefore I have omitted Tablet XII from the translation and from further consideration.

‡ The textual tradition is actually far more complex. The content and wording of the Old Babylonian and Neo-Babylonian texts from Uruk may represent a tradition distinct from that of the Middle Babylonian, Neo-Assyrian, and Neo-Babylonian tablets from Babylon.

from other literature to new purposes. The Standard Version was based on an earlier Epic of Gilgamesh that was first composed in the Old Babylonian period (1800–1600 B.C.) and that seems to have soon existed in two or more variants. The remains of the Old Babylonian tablets are fragmentary but extremely interesting, for they are often markedly different in content and style from the Standard Version of the same episodes. Between these fall the various fragments dating to the Middle Babylonian period, which come not only from Mesopotamia proper but also from other areas adopting cuneiform: Anatolia, Syria, and Canaan. In Anatolia the Epic was also adapted or translated into Hurrian and Hittite.*

The original Epic of Gilgamesh composed in the Old Babylonian period was not an act of pure imagination, nor does it seem to have derived from ancient folktales. Just as the author of the Standard Version rewrote the earlier Old Babylonian epic, imbuing it with his own insights and concerns, so too the Old Babylonian author had created his Epic from prior written literature. In good Mesopotamian scholarly tradition, the Old Babylonian author drew heavily on the written literary corpus which provided the "raw material" for his grander effort. There existed a number of independent, short heroic tales in the Sumerian language about Gilgamesh; they did not form a connected cycle, nor is there a major unifying theme such as the fear of death. In addition to these Sumerian tales, the Old Babylonian author incorporated themes from a variety of other myths unrelated to Gilgamesh. These "literary antecedents" to the Epic of Gilgamesh are worth describing, both for their intrinsic interest as the earliest Gilgamesh traditions known, and for what they reveal about the process of literary creation. Comparison of these original source texts with the integrated Epic reveals the power of transformation of the creative mind.

The Sumerian Epics

It is assumed that stories about the deeds of the famous King of Uruk, Gilgamesh, circulated in his own time, ca. 2700 B.C. It is possible that within several generations his exploits were already written

---

* Tigay, *Evolution,* is the best source for the reader interested in more detail about the various versions. See particularly pp. 39–109 for the differences between the Old Babylonian and Standard versions, and pp. 110–29 for the Middle Babylonian fragments. The find-spots and dates of the tablets are on pp. 130–31. More recently, Middle and Neo-Babylonian fragments have been published. Early reports of the name "Gilgamesh" in tablets from Ebla (Tigay, p. 16, n. 65) have since been retracted.

down, but of this we have so far no tangible evidence.* The earliest *written* epics about Gilgamesh were produced in the Sumerian language during the reign of King Shulgi of the Third Dynasty of Ur (Ur III), ca. 2000 B.C. He had claimed the gods and ancient kings of Uruk as his ancestors to strengthen the legitimacy of his kingship. In hymns written in Shulgi's honor he is called the son of Ninsun and Lugalbanda, and he refers to himself as the "brother and friend" of Gilgamesh. As the translator notes, one hymn seems to contain a lengthy dialogue between Shulgi and Gilgamesh, in which the divine brothers alternate in singing each other's praise and glory.† It is likely that Shulgi also commissioned the writing of the epics about his ancestors, and that they were significantly colored by his ambitions as king—i.e., they were not simply the recording of authentic oral tradition but were consciously composed, with perhaps only a core of some historical deed.‡

No tablets with these Sumerian epics actually date to the stage of composition in the Ur III period. They exist in later copies made for scribal practice and libraries during the Old Babylonian period, by which time several different versions had evolved in the scribal circles local to each city. Some versions are more elaborated, others have contradictory details or emphasis. Below I briefly summarize those fragments of the Sumerian epics discovered to date.

"Gilgamesh and Agga."§ This short "epic" of only 115 lines tells of a curious confrontation between Agga of Kish, son of Enmebaragessi, and King Gilgamesh of Uruk. Agga sends his envoys to enforce his sovereignty. Gilgamesh puts the matter to the city Elders, who refuse to resist, but the Young Men (the able-bodied) agree in order to escape conscription into Agga's army. Gilgamesh has Enkidu organize the troops and fashion a "terrifying aura" to ensure victory. When Agga arrives, Uruk panics. A volunteer goes to meet Agga; when an officer of Uruk walks along the city wall Agga asks if that man is his master.

---

* There are grounds for hope, though: in the last fifteen years several very early literary texts have been found at Abu-Salabikh dating to the Fara period (ca. 2500 B.C.), including a fragment telling of an adventure of Lugalbanda, Gilgamesh's father. See Claus Wilcke, "Lugalbanda," in *RealLexikon der Assyriologie*, vol. 7 (1987), p. 130, section 4.1.4.

† Jacob Klein, *The Royal Hymns of Shulgi, King of Ur: Man's Quest for Immortal Fame* (Transactions of the American Philosophical Society, vol. 71, part 7, 1981), p. 10.

‡ For example, the early Fara period Lugalbanda epic mentioned above shares with the Lugalbanda epics composed under Shulgi a basic theme—a journey through the mountains—but otherwise seems basically a different story.

§ See Jerrold Cooper in *Journal of Cuneiform Studies*, vol. 33 (1981), pp. 224–41, and Jacob Klein, "The Capture of Agga by Gilgames," *Journal of the American Oriental Society*, vol. 103 (1983), pp. 200–204.

He replies negatively, adding that Gilgamesh's very appearance would instantly cause Agga's capture. This insolent threat is met by a beating. Then Gilgamesh in his "terrifying aura" mounts the wall, and Enkidu goes out to Agga, who again asks if that man is his master. Enkidu replies affirmatively and, as forewarned, Agga's army suffers instant defeat and Agga is captured in the middle of his army. The conclusion is curious—Gilgamesh recalls that once Agga had spared him, and since Agga now humbles himself, Gilgamesh releases him.

The only apparent echoes of this tale in the Akkadian Epic of Gilgamesh seem to be the consultations with the Elders and the Young Men in Tablets II and III, and Gilgamesh's magnanimous desire to release the defeated Humbaba in Tablet V.

"Gilgamesh and Huwawa (Humbaba)."* Also known as "Gilgamesh and the Cedar Forest," this work is known in two very different versions, a long one of 200+ lines, and a short one of only 84+ lines. This is the epic with the widest textual variation, known from at least four cities.

Seeing a body floating down the river, Gilgamesh feels his first fear of death. Anticipating his personal mortality, he proposes to his servant, Enkidu, a heroic campaign against Huwawa, the monstrous Guardian of the Cedar Forest, which would ensure him the immortality of fame. Gilgamesh enlists the Sun God's assistance in the form of seven demons who are to direct his boat upstream to Huwawa. Then fifty men are selected to accompany them, and weapons are prepared. During the voyage they cross seven mountains. When they reach Huwawa's dwelling in the Cedar Forest, Gilgamesh spontaneously cuts down a cedar tree. In a rage Huwawa puts on his protective auras; Gilgamesh is overcome and sits stunned, experiencing fearsome visions. In one version, Gilgamesh describes the ominous dreams but Enkidu urges him to go on; in the other, it is Enkidu who describes the awful dreams and then tries to dissuade Gilgamesh from going on. Gilgamesh disarms Huwawa by a ruse, claiming that he wants to become a part of Huwawa's folk. In one version he tricks Huwawa into giving up his protective auras by offering him his sisters; in the other he offers Huwawa costly gifts, including the finest foods and precious

---

* See D. O. Edzard, "Literatur," in *RealLexikon der Assyriologie*, vol. 7 (1987), p. 40; and Aaron Shaffer, "Gilgamesh, the Cedar Forest, and Mesopotamian History," *Journal of the American Oriental Society*, vol. 103 (1983), pp. 307–13, where the differences between the two main versions are stressed.

stones, for each of the seven auras. Disarmed and betrayed, Huwawa is finally shackled like a beast. But Gilgamesh takes pity on him and would free him, even to the point of taking him on as an ally. Enkidu opposes this, and eventually kills Huwawa, puts his head in a sack, and presents it to the chief god Enlil. Enlil curses the two of them with seven curses for killing the divinely appointed Guardian of the Cedar Forest, and he distributes the seven auras to nature.

This epic is the basis for Tablets IV and V of the Standard Version.

"Gilgamesh and the Bull of Heaven." * The epic is very poorly preserved, with one main tablet of 144 + lines and a couple of small fragments. All that remains of the main tablet is the bottom half; the beginning, a large part of the middle, and the end are missing. One presumes that the missing beginning gives the reasons for Inanna's anger toward Gilgamesh. When the text begins Inanna refuses to allow Gilgamesh to administer justice in her sanctuary; this may be one of the reasons he turned against her. Inanna demands the Bull of Heaven from her father, Anu; he at first refuses, but she threatens to cry out to all the other gods of the universe. Out of fear Anu changes his mind and hands over the Bull, and Inanna sends it to Uruk. When the text resumes the Bull is in Uruk; Gilgamesh and Enkidu talk, and then both probably kill the Bull. The end is missing.

This is the source for Tablet VI of the Standard Version. This entire episode was probably not included in the original Old Babylonian epic, where the motivation for Enkidu's death was only his killing of Humbaba, not the slaying of the Bull. The episode was already part of the Epic in the Middle Babylonian period.

"Gilgamesh in the Netherworld." † Sometimes called "The Death of Gilgamesh," this fragment is very poorly preserved, only 135 + lines of an original 450. Some readable lines of this "death lament" do echo the central themes of the later Epic. One passage states: "The great mountain Enlil, the father of the gods, . . . decreed kingship as Gilgamesh's destiny, but did not decree for him eternal life." Later it is said: "He lay on the bed of destined fate, unable to get up."

In addition to these fragments in which Gilgamesh figures, the Akkadian Epic also draws on other traditional Sumerian literary motifs

---

* See Adam Falkenstein, "Gilgameš," in *RealLexikon der Assyriologie*, vol. 3 (1957–71), p. 361.
† See the translation by Samuel Noah Kramer in *Ancient Near Eastern Texts Relating to the Old Testament* (3d ed.; Princeton, N.J., 1969), pp. 50–52.

not originally connected with Gilgamesh. The early life of Enkidu (Tablet I) seems to be modeled on the portrayal of primitive man as found in the Sumerian text called "Lahar and Ashnan": "Mankind of that time knew not the eating of bread, knew not the wearing of garments. The people went around with skins on their bodies, drank water from ditches." By the same token, the creation of Enkidu by the mother goddess (Tablet I) clearly derives from some Sumerian creation motifs or text not yet discovered.*

The Flood Story and Utanapishtim

In addition to the various Sumerian texts just mentioned, the Standard Version of the Epic of Gilgamesh incorporates part of another composition not originally related to Gilgamesh, the Akkadian "Myth of Atrahasis." In Tablet XI Gilgamesh asks Utanapishtim how he, to all appearances a normal human being, attained eternal life like a god. Utanapishtim then recites "a hidden thing, a secret of the gods," the story of how he survived the Flood. His account is taken from the long "Myth of Atrahasis," composed ca. 1600 B.C., which tells of the creation of man, several attempts by the gods to exterminate mankind because of noise and overpopulation, and a final Flood survived by only Atrahasis (Utanapishtim) and his family. The story Utanapishtim tells Gilgamesh is clearly only an abstract from the longer myth, where there is a lengthy justification building up to the final, exterminating Flood. Utanapishtim omits all of this and begins where he becomes involved, presenting the Flood as a mere whim of the gods: "Their hearts carried the great gods to inflict the Flood." The recitation of the Flood Story, however, in no way advances the movement of the Epic; it is a lengthy digression from Gilgamesh's quest, included only for its narrative interest. Note that Utanapishtim had already at the end of Tablet X revealed the true "secret of the gods," i.e. that the gods had established a limited lifetime for all mankind, and unending death. (The original Old Babylonian version of the Epic of Gilgamesh surely contained only this brief allusion to the Flood Story.) The account of the Flood itself is not well preserved in the original "Myth of Atrahasis" but is complete in the Epic of Gilgamesh.†

* See Tigay, *Evolution*, pp. 198–213 and 192–97, respectively.
† See the translation by W. G. Lambert and A. R. Millard, *Atra-hasis. The Babylonian Story of the Flood* (Oxford, 1969). New pieces of the myth have been published

There is another aspect to the character of Utanapishtim in the Standard Version that is not found in the "Myth of Atrahasis": his role as dispenser of wisdom. This was the primary role of his predecessor in the Sumerian tradition, who is known by his Sumerian name Ziusudra ("Life of Long Days"). Only very recently has there come to light another Sumerian text—very fragmentary—that refers to Ziusudra as the recipient of eternal life, and death as the lot of the rest of mankind: "[Etana?], the king, . . . the man who ascended to heaven, . . . like Ziusudra sought for life . . ." and later "death is the share of mankind." *

In sum, it is clear that the author of the Epic of Gilgamesh was a scholar, steeped in the written traditions of Mesopotamia.

The Historical Gilgamesh

There is no doubt that Gilgamesh was a real historical figure who ruled the city of Uruk at the end of the Early Dynastic II period (ca. 2700–2500 B.C.). Though no royal inscriptions are known that would directly establish his existence, one person he is associated with in epic is actually attested by contemporary inscriptions. The Sumerian epic "Gilgamesh and Agga," mentioned earlier, refers to a war fought between Gilgamesh of Uruk and Agga of the city of Kish, son of Enmebaragessi. This Enmebaragessi is a historically authenticated figure, with two contemporary inscriptions. It may be merely a matter of time and luck before archaeologists uncover an inscription of his near contemporary, Gilgamesh.

In Sumerian the name was originally Bilgamesh; the earliest writing with initial "G" is in an Old Babylonian omen text. (Gilgamesh is now the long-established conventional form.) The name is similar in formation to other authentic personal names of the Early Dynastic period and may mean "The Old One Is Youthful." † Such a meaning is inherently unlikely for a name given at birth, so it may have been given at his coronation. The earliest written attestation of the name is in a list of gods dating to the end of the Early Dynastic II period where the deified Gilgamesh occurs next to the deified Lugalbanda. Shortly there-

---

since then; a complete copy of the myth recently discovered at the site of Sippar has not yet been published.

* See Bendt Alster, "A Sumerian Poem About Early Rulers," *Acta Sumerologica* (Tokyo), vol. 8 (1986), pp. 1–9; the translations are of Bii4–5 and 19.

† The interpretation of the name is by Adam Falkenstein in his article "Gilgameš" (cited earlier), p. 357.

after the deified ancestor Gilgamesh is occasionally found as an element in Sumerian personal names and in Akkadian personal names from Susa, in Elam.

According to the tradition of literary texts, Lugalbanda and his wife Ninsun were Gilgamesh's parents. The Sumerian King List, however, has Lugalbanda preceding Gilgamesh as ruler of Uruk by two, and says that Gilgamesh's father was a *"lillu*-spirit, a high priest of Kulaba." (This may be the origin of the description of Gilgamesh in the Epic as two-thirds god.) Texts also name a son of Gilgamesh, Urlugal (or Urnungal), and a grandson, Udulkalama—though the Standard Version of the Epic makes no mention of them, as we noted earlier.

In literary texts Gilgamesh is variously identified by the title "lord," "great lord," and "lord of Kulaba" (Kulaba was the quarter of the city of Uruk where the ancient Ziggurat was located). A major expansion of the Ziggurat, along with the building of the wall of Uruk, was traditionally identified with Gilgamesh, although the earliest inscription claiming that Gilgamesh built the wall of Uruk dates only as far back as King Anam of Uruk, ca. 1800 B.C. The principal political achievement of Gilgamesh's reign, as seen in later Ur III tradition, was the victory over the king of Kish by which Gilgamesh "brought over the kingship [that is, the political supremacy in Mesopotamia] from Kish to Uruk."[*] The Sumerian King List reports that transfer in its usual laconic style: "Kish was smitten with weapons, its kingship was carried to Eanna [the Temple of Uruk]."

Offerings were made to Gilgamesh as a divinized ancestor and hero from the late Early Dynastic period to about the end of the Ur III period, though we know nothing of the nature of the cult.[†] We have seen King Shulgi's close identification with Uruk and its lineage, and it may be that he commissioned the Sumerian Gilgamesh epics. Nonetheless, after the demise of his dynasty, official royal support for the cult of Gilgamesh faded. Yet it may be that this loss of political sponsorship allowed the now purely "literary Gilgamesh" to fire the imagination of an Old Babylonian writer. Ironically, Gilgamesh found the fame and

[*] See Klein, *The Royal Hymns of Shulgi* (cited earlier), p. 10.
[†] A short text of this period called "The Death of Urnammu" refers to Gilgamesh as Lord of the Netherworld, a role elaborated later, particularly in Assyria. This may account for the addition of Tablet XII, dealing with conditions in the Netherworld, to the eleven-tablet Epic. See W. G. Lambert, "Gilgameš in Religious, Historical, and Omen Texts and the Historicity of Gilgameš," in Paul Garelli, ed., *Gilgamesh et sa légende* (Paris, 1960), pp. 39–53.

immortality he so desperately sought the more removed he became from his historical identity.

Reflections of the Epic in Mesopotamian Culture

The Epic was clearly known widely in antiquity—in cities throughout Mesopotamia for some 1,500 years, and in Anatolia and Syria-Palestine at least during the mid-second millennium. Nonetheless, its fame was probably limited to the ranks of those literate in cuneiform writing. For all its dramatic and human qualities, the Epic does not seem to have become a byword in the land, to have generated any "classic" expressions in the language. No king claims that he is as wise or brave or strong "as Gilgamesh." In letters no one invokes Gilgamesh and Enkidu as the paradigm of friendship. This is not to say that Gilgamesh was unknown outside scribal circles; but the by-products of the Epic in the general culture of Mesopotamia are few, limited to allusions in a few scholarly writings (divinatory texts and a political propaganda letter) and some representations in art.

In 1957 a document was published that identified itself as a "message from Gilgamesh, the mighty king, who has no rival." Addressed to a king (name and city are broken), the letter makes a second demand that the king send enormous quantities of animals, foods, and precious metals and stones to "Gilgamesh" for a monument to "my friend, Enkidu." This extraordinary composition, found in three copies (at Sultantepe in southeast Turkey), dates to the Neo-Assyrian period and was composed by a native Assyrian court scribe. The letter also includes allusions to two other Gilgamesh traditions (the Sumerian King List and omens) and may be a piece of political allegory, or possibly a satire. Such fictive letters from gods or other notables are a distinct Mesopotamian literary genre; though it contains nothing new about either the historical or the legendary Gilgamesh, the letter does evidence a certain vitality of the Gilgamesh legend as late as the first millennium.*

In spite of the fame of the Epic, remarkably few echoes of it are to be found in art.† Faces of Humbaba are fairly frequent, but most are

---

* See the article by F. R. Kraus, "Der Brief des Gilgameš," *Anatolian Studies*, vol. 30 (1980), pp. 109–21.

† See Lambert, "Gilgamesh in Literature and Art" (with many illustrations), and Collon, *First Impressions*, pp. 178ff. Note especially that the large wall reliefs from Dur-

FIGURE 2. A clay mask of Humbaba. The "head of Humbaba" appears often in Mesopotamian art as a fearsome protective demon, as here, with teeth bared in a wide, gnashing grimace. The face of Humbaba was the prototype of the Gorgon head in archaic Greek art. Clay mask from Ur, U2685, photo reproduced with the permission of the University Museum, University of Pennsylvania.

FIGURE 3. The slaying of Humbaba. An impression of a Neo-Assyrian period cylinder seal, reproduced with the permission of Dr. Leonard Gorelick.

FIGURE 4. The slaying of Humbaba. An impression of a section of a Mitanni period (ca. 1500–1400 B.C.) cylinder seal showing a more schematized version of the episode than the one in Figure 3. BM 89569, reproduced by courtesy of the Trustees of the British Museum.

probably related to his function as a protective "demon" rather than to his specific role in the Epic of Gilgamesh. (See Figure 2.) The one episode from the Epic that can be identified in art with some confidence and frequency is the killing of Humbaba by Gilgamesh and Enkidu (Tablet V). This appears on several Old Babylonian clay plaques, and on some two dozen cylinder seals, decorative objects, and stone reliefs from the fifteenth to fifth centuries B.C. The basic scene shows Humbaba down on one knee, while Gilgamesh on the left thrusts his dagger at Humbaba's neck, and Enkidu on the right holds Humbaba and brandishes a weapon. (See Figures 3 and 4.) The killing of the Bull of Heaven is represented on a few cylinder seals from the mid-second millennium to the seventh century B.C. The Bull of Heaven is shown as

Sharrukin showing two heroes, one with a lion, are not (as sometimes proposed) Gilgamesh and Enkidu, but rather protective demons. See Lambert, p. 51, and the F. A. M. Wiggerman article (pp. 100 and 102) cited by Lambert, p. 38, n. 5.

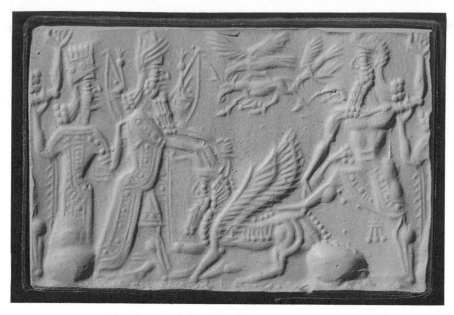

FIGURE 5. The slaying of the Bull of Heaven. Ishtar is shown trying to stop Gilgamesh and Enkidu from killing the Bull. Collon, *First Impressions*, p. 181 (no. 858), dates the seal to the Neo-Babylonian period. BM 89435, reproduced by courtesy of the Trustees of the British Museum.

a bull with wings. As in the killing of Humbaba, Gilgamesh on the left holds the Bull and thrusts his dagger into its neck, while Enkidu holds it by the tail or wing. (See Figure 5.)

The Fate of Gilgamesh

The latest cuneiform fragment of the Epic dates to the first century B.C. With the gradual demise of cuneiform writing and the traditions carried by it, the Epic of Gilgamesh fell into oblivion, for virtually none of Mesopotamian literature was translated into other languages.

There was interest among Hellenistic Greeks in the ancient history of Mesopotamia, but not in the native Mesopotamian form. For example, Berossus, a priest of Babylon and probably a court astrologer under Antiochus I (280–261 B.C.), wrote in Greek of "the histories of heaven (and earth) and sea and the first birth and the kings and their deeds." Although he used original cuneiform documents (king lists, myths, chronicles, etc.) as sources, they were not themselves presented but their historical content was abstracted and woven together into a descriptive narrative. Gilgamesh probably received no more than the standard citation of name and the length of reign, with perhaps a brief remark about his deeds.*

More puzzling is the lack of references to Gilgamesh in the Syro-Phoenician cultures of the first millennium, since cuneiform and its literature had been widely known in this area in the late second millennium. Akkadian had become the language of international diplomacy in the fourteenth century B.C., used in court chanceries and schools with traditional scribal curricula. A piece of Gilgamesh (Tablet VII, Enkidu's death; probably a scribal practice tablet) was even found at Megiddo, in Canaan, and another at Emar, in Syria. The Hebrew Bible has allusions to other persons or themes that were derived ultimately from Mesopotamian sources, most obviously the Flood Story, but Gilgamesh is not among them.†

There are two possible allusions to Gilgamesh in non-cuneiform sources—with the usual *caveat* "so far."‡ In a first century B.C. Aramaic Book of Giants found among the Dead Sea Scrolls from Qumran the names (of the giants) glgmys/š and hwbbš appear in very fragmentary contexts. It is speculated that these may be Gilgamesh and Humbaba. The Book of Giants became very well known as part of the writings of Manichaeism, and was translated into many languages of Asia; a Middle Persian fragment preserves the name of the giant thought to be Humbaba.

There remains one very uncertain allusion in a non-cuneiform source. The seventh-century Nestorian Christian Theodor Bar Qoni, writing in Syriac, produced material for teaching religion in which he

---

* A convenient translation of what remains of Berossus's three-book history is Stanley Mayer Burstein, *The Babyloniaca of Berossus* (Malibu, Calif.: Undena Publications, 1978). Berossus's purpose in writing his history is discussed on pp. 6–8.

† The cultural borrowings between Syria-Palestine and Mesopotamia—in both directions—are described by W. G. Lambert in "The Interchange of Ideas Between Southern Mesopotamia and Syria-Palestine as Seen in Literature," in Hans-Jörg Nissen and Johannes Renger, eds., *Mesopotamien und seine Nachbarn* (Berlin: Dietrich Reimer Verlag, 1982), pp. 311–16. Lambert states that "the Babylonian material transformed and embedded in Genesis 1–11 reached Syria-Palestine in the Amarna period [fourteenth century], became local oral tradition in this area, and in this form eventually reached the Israelites" (p. 315).

‡ See Tigay, *Evolution*, p. 252–55. The story in Aelian's "On Animals" is almost certainly a late transference to Gilgamesh and thus not an echo of an authentic tradition.

lists among the kings after the Flood one "Ganmagos, and in the days of this latter Abraham was born in Ur of the Chaldeans." Some scholars have proposed that Ganmagos might be Gilgamesh. If so, it is the latest surviving mention of Gilgamesh until the rediscovery and decipherment of cuneiform in the nineteenth century.

A CHRONOLOGY OF THE GILGAMESH EPIC

B.C.	2700	Lugalbanda(?), Gilgamesh of Uruk	Early Dynastic II period (2700–2500) Fara, Abu-Salabikh tablets
	2500	Epic about Lugalbanda	Early Dynastic III period (2500–2350)
	2300		Akkad period (2350–2200); Sargon of Akkad
	2100	Sumerian epics composed	Third Dynasty of Ur (2100–2000); King Shulgi
	1800	earliest tablets of Sumerian epics	Old Babylonian period (1800–1600); Hammurabi
	1700	Akkadian Epic composed: Old Babylonian version	
	1600		Middle Babylonian period (1600–1000)
	1500	Middle Babylonian version; Hurrian, Hittite translations	
	1300	Sinleqqiunninni, "author" of Standard Version	
	1000		Neo-Assyrian period (1000–612) Neo- & Late-Babylonian periods (1000–125)
	800	oldest tablets of Standard Version	
	700	royal libraries at Nineveh	Aramaic replacing Akkadian
	500	earliest Neo-Babylonian copies	
	200	latest copy of Gilgamesh Epic	
	100	"Gilgamesh," "Humbaba" (?) in Book of Giants	
A.D.	100		latest dated cuneiform tablet
	600	"Ganmagos" in Syriac scholia	

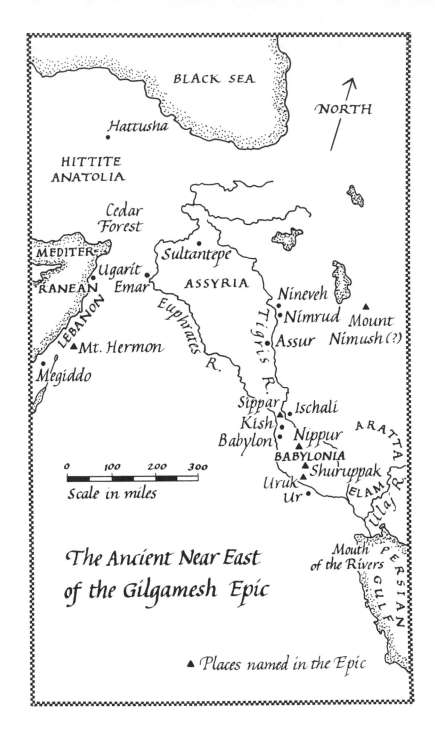

The Ancient Near East
of the Gilgamesh Epic

▲ Places named in the Epic

The Epic of Gilgamesh

TABLET

I

The Epic opens with an introductory scene, establishing the context in which the story of Gilgamesh comes to be told. A narrator serving as guide walks through the city of Uruk proclaiming to a visitor (actually, the reader of the Epic) the profound wisdom of "the one who experienced all things," who learned the secret of the gods from the time "before the Flood." The narrator exhorts his companion to examine the monuments this extraordinary king created: the incomparable Temple of Anu and Ishtar, the massive wall enclosing the vast area of the city, and the lapis lazuli inscription that he buried in the wall's foundation for future generations, the text of the Epic itself.

It begins with a hymn in praise of Gilgamesh, a king of bold deeds, beauty, and semidivine ancestry. Yet after a short break in the text, Gilgamesh is described as oppressing the men and young women of Uruk in some still uncertain way, perhaps by forcing the men into hopeless contests of strength and taking some sexual advantage of the women. The chief god of Uruk, hearing the pleas of the people for relief, had the mother goddess create a rival to challenge Gilgamesh, the primitive Enkidu, at one with nature. These super- and subhuman counterparts enact a classic confrontation of civilization against nature.

A trapper determines to get rid of Enkidu, who has been setting free all the wild animals caught in his traps. Gilgamesh advises him to take a temple harlot to Enkidu in the wild, for after sexual intercourse Enkidu will be rejected by the world of nature and no longer a threat to the trapper. Enkidu then accepts the harlot's suggestion to go to Uruk, expecting to meet Gilgamesh and by his sheer strength to put an end to his oppression. Meanwhile, Gilgamesh has had two dreams, which his mother interprets as the arrival of one who at first will be a competitor, but who in the end will become his intimate friend.

The Standard Version text of Tablet I is almost complete, except for the opening lines and a few others. Though Tablet I of the Old Babylonian version is not extant, we know that it began at line 28 with the traditional royal hymn of praise. The narrator's opening lines were added by a later author who wanted to impart very different values, honoring not Gilgamesh's adventures but his achievement of understanding and humanity.

TABLET I

The Legacy

1 He who has seen everything, *I will make known* (?) to the lands.
I will teach (?) about him who experienced all things,
. . . alike,
Anu granted him the totality of knowledge of *all*.
He saw the Secret, discovered the Hidden,
he brought information of (the time) before the Flood.
He went on a distant journey, pushing himself to exhaustion,
but then was brought to peace.
He carved on a stone stela all of his toils,
and built the wall of Uruk-Haven,[1]
the wall of the sacred Eanna Temple, the holy sanctuary.
Look at its wall which gleams like *copper*(?),
inspect its inner wall, the likes of which no one can equal!
Take hold of the threshold stone—it dates from ancient times!
Go close to the Eanna Temple, the residence of Ishtar,
such as no later king or man ever equaled!
17 Go up on the wall of Uruk and walk around,
examine its foundation, inspect its brickwork thoroughly.
Is not (even the core of) the brick structure made of kiln-fired brick,
and did not the Seven Sages themselves lay out its plans?
One league city, one league palm gardens, one league lowlands, the
open area(?) of the Ishtar Temple,
three leagues and the open area(?) of Uruk it (the wall) encloses.
23 Find the copper tablet box,
open the . . . of its lock of bronze,

1. In the Standard Version the city's common epithet is literally "Uruk-the-(sheep)
Enclosure" or "Uruk-the-Sheepfold." I prefer to translate the notion of a safe refuge for
the weak as "Uruk-Haven." In the Old Babylonian Version the city is characterized as
"Uruk-of-the-City Squares," often rendered as "Broad-Marted Uruk."

undo the fastening of its secret opening.
Take and read out from the lapis lazuli tablet
how Gilgamesh went through every hardship.

Gilgamesh

28 Supreme over other kings, lordly in appearance,
he is the hero, born of Uruk, the goring wild bull.
He walks out in front, the leader,
and walks at the rear, trusted by his companions.
Mighty net, protector of his people,
raging flood-wave who destroys even walls of stone!
Offspring of Lugalbanda, Gilgamesh is strong to perfection,
son of the august cow, Rimat-Ninsun, . . . Gilgamesh is awesome to
                                                            perfection.
It was he who opened the mountain passes,
who dug wells on the flank of the mountain.
It was he who crossed the ocean, the vast seas, to the rising sun,
who explored the world regions, seeking life.
It was he who reached by his own sheer strength Utanapishtim, the
                                                            Faraway,
who restored the sanctuaries (or: cities) that the Flood had destroyed!
. . . for teeming mankind.
Who can compare with him in kingliness?
Who can say like Gilgamesh: "I am King!"?
Whose name, from the day of his birth, was called "Gilgamesh"?
46 Two-thirds of him is god, one-third of him is human.
The Great Goddess [Aruru] designed(?) the model for his body,
she prepared his form . . .
. . . beautiful, handsomest of men,
. . . perfect . . .
. . .
He walks around in the enclosure of Uruk,
like a wild bull he makes himself mighty, head raised (over others).
There is no rival who can raise his weapon against him.
His fellows stand (at the alert), attentive to his (orders ?),

and the men of Uruk become anxious in . . .
Gilgamesh does not leave a son to his father,
day and night he *arrogantly*(?) . . .
[The following lines are interpreted as rhetorical, perhaps spoken by the oppressed citizens of Uruk.]
Is Gilgamesh the shepherd of Uruk-Haven,
is he the shepherd . . .
bold, eminent, knowing, and *wise*?
Gilgamesh does not leave a girl to *her mother*(?)![2]
63 The daughter of the warrior, the bride of the young man,
the gods kept hearing their complaints, so
the gods of the heavens implored the Lord of Uruk [Anu]:
"You have indeed brought into being a mighty wild bull, head
raised!
There is no rival who can raise a weapon against him.
His fellows stand (at the alert), attentive to his (orders ?),
Gilgamesh does not leave a son to his father,
day and night he arrogantly . . .
Is he the shepherd of Uruk-Haven,
is he their shepherd . . .
bold, eminent, knowing, and *wise*?
Gilgamesh does not leave a girl to *her mother*(?)!"

Enkidu

75 The daughter of the warrior, the bride of the young man,
Anu listened to their complaints,
and (the gods) called out to Aruru:
"It was you, Aruru, who created *mankind*(?),[3]
now create a *zikru*[4] to it/him.
Let him be equal to his (Gilgamesh's) stormy heart,

2. Or "to *her betrothed*(?)."
3. Or "*Gilgamesh* (?)."
4. The Akkadian *zikru* normally means "what was ordered, commanded" or "reply, response"; neither sense really gives a clear meaning. Perhaps in these lines and VIII, 228, *zikru* may have another meaning. Whatever the sense, *zikru* is probably also a pun echoing Enkidu as the *kisru* "meteorite(?)" (of Anu) later in Tablet I.

let them be a match for each other so that Uruk may find
peace!"
82 When Aruru heard this she created within herself the *zikru* of Anu.
Aruru washed her hands, she pinched off some clay, and threw it into
the wilderness.
In the wilderness(?) she created valiant Enkidu,
born of Silence, endowed with strength by Ninurta.
His whole body was shaggy with hair,
he had a full head of hair like a woman,
his locks billowed in profusion like Ashnan.[5]
He knew neither people nor settled living,
but wore a garment like Sumukan.[6]
He ate grasses with the gazelles,
and jostled at the watering hole with the animals;
as with animals, his thirst was slaked with (mere) water.

The Trapper and the Harlot

94 A notorious trapper[7]
came face-to-face with him opposite the watering hole.
A first, a second, and a third day
he came face-to-face with him opposite the watering hole.
On seeing him the trapper's face went stark with fear,
and he (Enkidu?) and his animals drew back home (?).
He was rigid with fear; though stock-still
his heart pounded and his face drained of color.
He was miserable to the core,
and his face looked like one who had made a long journey.
104 The trapper addressed his father saying:[8]

5. Ashnan, the goddess of grain, was portrayed with hair of billowing grain.
6. Sumukan was the god of wild animals. Enkidu was clothed in animal skins.
7. The word is commonly translated "hunter," but "trapper" seems more accurate here because the animals are captured in traps or pits, not killed by weapons. There is a play on words with the derogatory epithet *habilu* ("notorious, despicable") and a homonym which is a rare term for "trapper."
8. This is the first of many occurrences of the stock phrases introducing direct speech, translated variously by the formal "addressed . . . saying" or "spoke . . . saying." The phrase is used only in literature.

"Father, a certain fellow has come from the mountains.
He is the mightiest in the land,
his strength is as mighty as the meteorite(?) of Anu![9]
He continually goes over the mountains,
he continually jostles at the watering place with the animals,
he continually plants his feet opposite the watering place.
I was afraid, so I did not go up to him.
He filled in the pits that I had dug,
wrenched out my traps that I had spread,
released from my grasp the wild animals.
He does not let me make my rounds in the wilderness!"

116 The trapper's father spoke to him saying:
"My son, there lives in Uruk a certain Gilgamesh.
There is no one stronger than he,
he is as strong as the meteorite(?) of Anu.
Go, set off to *Uruk*,
tell Gilgamesh of this Man of Might.
He will give you the harlot Shamhat, take *her with you*.
The woman will overcome the fellow (?) as if she were strong.
When the animals are drinking at the watering place
have her take off her robe and expose her sex.
When he sees her he will draw near to her,
and his animals, who grew up in his wilderness, will be alien
to him."

128 He heeded his father's advice.
The trapper went off *to Uruk*,
he made the journey, stood inside of Uruk,
and declared to . . . Gilgamesh:
"There is a certain fellow who has come from the mountains—

9. The Akkadian words *kisru ša Anu* are very difficult. Anu was the sky god, and the word *kisru* has a number of possible meanings in different contexts, including "lump of metal" and "a celestial phenomenon." Later in Tablet I, 227ff., the "*kisru* of Anu" is a heavy object that falls from the starry sky and remains intact on the ground, hence the tentative rendering "meteorite of Anu." Other proposals include "the vault of the heavens" and "concentration." See also the earlier note on *zikru*. The corresponding word in the original Old Babylonian version is damaged and is probably different, but there is no consensus on the restoration.

he is the mightiest in the land,
his strength is as mighty as the meteorite(?) of Anu!
He continually goes over the mountains,
he continually jostles at the watering place with the animals,
he continually plants his feet opposite the watering place.
I was afraid, so I did not go up to him.
He filled in the pits that I had dug,
wrenched out my traps that I had spread,
released from my grasp the wild animals.
He does not let me make my rounds in the wilderness!"

143 Gilgamesh said to the trapper:

"Go, trapper, bring the harlot, Shamhat, with you.
When the animals are drinking at the watering place
have her take off her robe and expose her sex.
When he sees her he will draw near to her,
and his animals, who grew up in his wilderness, will be alien
to him."

The Harlot

149 The trapper went, bringing the harlot, Shamhat, with him.
They set off on the journey, making direct way.
On the third day they arrived at the appointed place,
and the trapper and the harlot sat down at their posts(?).
A first day and a second they sat opposite the watering hole.
The animals arrived and drank at the watering hole,
the wild beasts arrived and slaked their thirst with water.
Then he, Enkidu, offspring of the mountains,
who eats grasses with the gazelles,
came to drink at the watering hole with the animals,
with the wild beasts he slaked his thirst with water.

160 Then Shamhat saw him—a primitive,
a savage fellow from the depths of the wilderness!

"That is he, Shamhat! Release your clenched arms,
expose your sex so he can take in your voluptuousness.
Do not be restrained—take his energy!

When he sees you he will draw near to you.
Spread out your robe so he can lie upon you,
and perform for this primitive the task of womankind!
His animals, who grew up in his wilderness, will become alien
                                                        to him,
and his lust will groan over you." [10]
170 Shamhat unclutched her bosom, exposed her sex, and he took in her
                                        voluptuousness.
She was not restrained, but took his energy.
She spread out her robe and he lay upon her,
she performed for the primitive the task of womankind.
His lust groaned over her;
for six days and seven nights Enkidu stayed aroused,
and had intercourse with the harlot
until he was sated with her charms.
But when he turned his attention to his animals,
the gazelles saw Enkidu and darted off,
the wild animals distanced themselves from his body.
181 Enkidu . . . his utterly depleted(?) body,
his knees that wanted to go off with his animals went rigid;
Enkidu was diminished, his running was not as before.
But then he drew himself up, for his understanding had broadened.
Turning around, he sat down at the harlot's feet,
gazing into her face, his ears attentive as the harlot spoke.
187 The harlot said to Enkidu:
    "You are beautiful,[11] Enkidu, you are become like a god.
    Why do you gallop around the wilderness with the wild beasts?
    Come, let me bring you into Uruk-Haven,
    to the Holy Temple, the residence of Anu and Ishtar,
    the place of Gilgamesh, who is wise to perfection,
    but who struts his power over the people like a wild bull."

10. The verb normally refers to quick repeated sounds made by animals (birds chirping, flies buzzing, cows lowing) and by water (bubbling or murmuring). In the context of lovemaking it could refer to grunting and groaning, and be a euphemism for sexual intercourse; the word is often translated "caress, embrace."
11. A recently published Akkadian fragment from Anatolia confirms the restoration "beautiful."

To Uruk

194 What she kept saying found favor with him.
Becoming aware of himself, he sought a friend.
Enkidu spoke to the harlot:
"Come, Shamhat, take me away with you
to the sacred Holy Temple, the residence of Anu and Ishtar,
the place of Gilgamesh, who is wise to perfection,
but who struts his power over the people like a wild bull.
I will challenge him . . .
Let me shout out in Uruk: 'I am the mighty one!'
Lead me in and I will change the order of things;
he whose strength is mightiest is the one born in the
wilderness!"

[Shamhat to Enkidu:]

205   "Come, let us go, so he may see your face.
I will lead you to Gilgamesh—I know where he will be.
Look about, Enkidu, inside Uruk-Haven,
where the people show off in skirted finery,
where every day is a day for some festival,
where the lyre(?) and drum play continually,
where harlots *stand about* prettily,
exuding voluptuousness, full of laughter,
and on the couch of night the sheets are spread (?).[12]

214   Enkidu, *you who do not know how* to live,
I will show you Gilgamesh, a man of extreme feelings (?).[13]
Look at him, gaze at his face—
he is a handsome youth, with freshness(?),
his entire body exudes voluptuousness.
He has mightier strength than you,
without sleeping day or night!

12. A new interpretation by Benjamin Foster ("Gilgamesh: Sex, Love and the Ascent of Knowledge," p. 29) is "They drive the Great Ones from their beds!" This, he explains, refers to "a well-known topos . . . wherein the 'Great Ones' retiring for the night is used as an image for the silence and loneliness of deep night."
13. The original means literally "happy-woeful man"—a man of changing moods?

Enkidu, it is your wrong thoughts you must change!
It is Gilgamesh whom Shamash loves,
and Anu, Enlil, and Ea have enlarged his mind.[14]
Even before you came from the mountain
Gilgamesh in Uruk had dreams about you."[15]

The Dreams

226 Gilgamesh got up and revealed the dream, saying to his mother:
"Mother, I had a dream last night.
Stars of the sky appeared,
and some kind of meteorite(?) of Anu fell next to me.
I tried to lift it but it was too mighty for me,
I tried to turn it over but I could not budge it.
The Land of Uruk was standing around it,
the whole land had assembled about it,
the populace was thronging around it,
the Men clustered about it,
and kissed its feet as if it were a little baby (?).
I loved it and embraced it as a wife.
I laid it down at your feet,
and you made it compete with me."

240 The mother of Gilgamesh, the wise, all-knowing, said to her Lord;
Rimat-Ninsun, the wise, all-knowing, said to Gilgamesh:
"As for the stars of the sky that appeared
and the meteorite(?) of Anu which fell next to you,
you tried to lift but it was too mighty for you,
you tried to turn it over but were unable to budge it,
you laid it down at my feet,
and I made it compete with you,
and *you loved* and embraced it as a wife."

14. Gilgamesh's special favor and intelligence were bestowed by the gods, whereas
Enkidu's "broadened understanding" (l. 184) was merely a result of human experience.
15. Gilgamesh's conversation with his mother about his dreams is presented as a
dialogue rather than as the harlot's narration. In the Old Babylonian version the two
dreams are far more distinct from each other; the Standard Version has conflated and
rearranged the elements from the dreams.

249   "*There will come to you* a mighty man, a comrade who saves
                                          his friend—

he is the mightiest in the land, he is strongest,
his strength is mighty as the meteorite(?) of Anu!
You loved him and embraced him as a wife;
and it is he who will repeatedly save you.
Your dream *is good and propitious*!"

255 A second time Gilgamesh said to his mother:
"Mother, I have had another dream:
At the gate of my marital chamber there lay an axe,
and people had collected about it.
The Land of Uruk was standing around it,
the whole land had assembled about it,
the populace was thronging around it.
I laid it down at your feet,
I loved it and embraced it as a wife,
and you made it compete with me."

265 The mother of Gilgamesh, the wise, all-knowing, said to her son;
Rimat-Ninsun, the wise, all-knowing, said to Gilgamesh:
"The axe that you saw (is) a man.
. . . (that) you love him and embrace as a wife,
but (that) I have compete with you."
[This means:]
"*There will come to you* a mighty man, a comrade who saves
                                          his friend—

he is the mightiest in the land, he is strongest,
he is as mighty as the meteorite(?) of Anu!"

273 Gilgamesh spoke to his mother saying:
"By the command of Enlil, the Great Counselor, so may it come
                                          to pass!

May I have a friend and adviser,
a friend and adviser may I have!
You have interpreted for me the dreams about him!"
After the harlot recounted *the dreams of Gilgamesh* to Enkidu
279 the two of them made love.

TABLET
II

Enkidu is gradually introduced to the ways of mankind by living with shepherds and protecting their flocks against wild animals, and by adopting the food, drink, and clothing of men. When he finally enters Uruk it is the time of a festival, during which Gilgamesh as king is to have intercourse with the "destined wife" first, before the husband. Enkidu is outraged by Gilgamesh's apparent licentious behavior, and attempts to block Gilgamesh from the "marital chamber." (There is much scholarly controversy over the correct reading and interpretation of these passages.) After a wrestling match in which Gilgamesh prevails, Enkidu acknowledges Gilgamesh as the legitimate superior and they become devoted friends, the first time either has felt true companionship. After some time, however, Enkidu softens with city life. Gilgamesh proposes an adventure that will achieve fame for himself and reinvigorate Enkidu's spirit and limbs: a journey to cut down the sacred Cedar Tree and to kill the Guardian of the Cedar Forest, Humbaba the Terrible. From his early years in the wilds Enkidu has known of the extreme danger associated with the ferocious Humbaba, whom the gods appointed Guardian. Even though Gilgamesh has special weapons made and apparently wins the support of the "men of Uruk," Enkidu remains fearful and tries to have the Elders dissuade Gilgamesh.

This tablet is not well preserved in the Standard Version. The translation has been restored heavily from the Old Babylonian version, though this results in some inconsistency in style and content.

TABLET II

Enkidu and the Harlot

1 Enkidu sits in front of her.

[The next 33 lines are missing; some of the fragmentary lines from 35 on are restored from parallels in the Old Babylonian.]

35 "Why . . ." (?)
His own counsel . . .
At his instruction . . .
Who knows his heart . . .
Shamhat pulled off her clothing,
and clothed him with one piece
while she clothed herself with a second.
She took hold of him as the gods do [1]
and brought him to the hut of the shepherds.

With the Shepherds

44 The shepherds gathered all around about him,
they marveled to themselves:
"How the youth resembles Gilgamesh—
tall in stature, towering up to the battlements over the wall!
Surely he was born in the mountains;
his strength is as mighty as the meteorite(?) of Anu!"
They placed food in front of him,
they placed beer in front of him;
Enkidu did not eat or drink, but squinted and stared.
. . .
Enkidu scattered the wolves, he chased away the lions.

1. Ur III and Old Babylonian period cylinder seals commonly show a goddess leading a worshipper by the hand into the presence of the chief god. For examples see Collon, *First Impressions*, nos. 114–18, 136, 153, 532–34. The Old Babylonian version reads, however, "like a child."

The herders could lie down in peace,
56 for Enkidu was their watchman.[2]

[The next 30 lines are missing in the Standard Version; lines 57–86 are taken from the Old Babylonian.]

. . . he made merry.
Then he raised his eyes and saw a man.
He said to the harlot:
"Shamhat, have that man go away!
Why has he come? I will call out his name!"
The harlot called out to the man
and went over to him and spoke with him.
"Young man, where are you hurrying?
Why this arduous pace?"
66 The young man spoke, saying to Enkidu:[3]
"They have invited me to a wedding,
as is the custom of the people.
. . . the selection(?) of brides(?) . . .

2. The parallel account in the Old Babylonian is more vivid:
Enkidu knew nothing about eating bread for food,
and of drinking beer he had not been taught.
The harlot spoke to Enkidu, saying:
"Eat the food, Enkidu, it is the way one lives.
Drink the beer, as is the custom of the land."
Enkidu ate the food until he was sated,
he drank the beer—seven jugs!—and became expansive and sang with joy!
He was elated and his face glowed.
He splashed his shaggy body with water,
and rubbed himself with oil, and turned into a human.
He put on some clothing and became like a warrior(?).
He took up his weapon and chased lions so that the shepherds could rest at
                                                                 night;
He routed the wolves, and chased off the lions.
With Enkidu as their guard, the herders could lie down.
A wakeful man, a singular youth, he was twice as tall (?) (as normal men).
3. The following passage is fairly well preserved in the Old Babylonian, but the in-
terpretation is much debated. It may refer to a normal marriage custom, except that
there is no other evidence of Mesopotamian kings having relations with brides before
the husbands do. The lines may mean that Gilgamesh's behavior was against custom,
and related to his wrongful taking of girls, as the citizens complained in I, 60–64. But
how then to reconcile its being "ordered by the counsel of Anu"? On the other hand, the
unique term "destined wife" (line 75) suggests that the scene may refer to the ancient
cultic practice called by scholars the "Sacred Marriage," a ritual act of intercourse origi-
nally associated with the coronation rite of the kings in Uruk. In the Ur III and early Old
Babylonian periods the cosmic Sacred Marriage of Inanna/Ishtar to Dumuzi/Tammuz

I have heaped up tasty delights for the wedding on the cere-
monial(?) platter.
For the King of Broad-Marted Uruk,
open is the veil(?) of the people for choosing (a girl).
For Gilgamesh, the King of Broad-Marted Uruk,
open is the veil(?) of the people for choosing.
He will have intercourse with the 'destined wife,'
he first, the husband afterward.
This is ordered by the counsel of Anu,
from the severing of his umbilical cord it has been destined
for him."
79 At the young man's speech his (Enkidu's) face flushed (with anger).
[Several lines are missing.]
Enkidu walked in front, and Shamhat after him.

The Contest

[The Standard Version resumes.]
87 He (Enkidu) walked down the street of Uruk-Haven,
. . . mighty . . .
He blocked the way through Uruk the Sheepfold.
The land of Uruk stood around him,
the whole land assembled about him,
the populace was thronging around him,
the men were clustered about him,
and kissed his feet as if he were a little baby(?).
95 Suddenly a handsome young man . . .⁴
For Ishara the bed of night(?)/marriage(?) is ready,

---

was reenacted by their human representative, a priestess and the king. Could ordinary
brides be selected for this role on occasion? If Gilgamesh's behavior is legitimate, is
Enkidu's anger due to misunderstanding or to jealousy? A newly discovered but still un-
published Old Babylonian tablet may soon clarify this provocative episode. The descrip-
tion of the celebrations taking place when Enkidu enters Uruk occupies eight complete
lines in the Old Babylonian but remains obscure; the author of the Standard Version
appears also not to have understood these archaic social practices, and has reduced the
scene to two lines (lines 96–97).
   4. The Old Babylonian is fuller, but still full of obscurity.
   In Uruk there were sacrifices continually,

for Gilgamesh as for a god a counterpart(?) is set up.
Enkidu blocked the entry to the marital chamber,
and would not allow Gilgamesh to be brought in.
They grappled with each other at the entry to the marital chamber,
in the street they attacked each other, the public square of the land.
102 The doorposts trembled and the wall shook,

[About 42 lines are missing from the Standard Version; lines 103–29 are taken from the Old Babylonian version.]

Gilgamesh bent his knees, with his other foot on the ground,
his anger abated and he turned his chest away.
After he turned his chest Enkidu said to Gilgamesh:
    "Your mother bore you ever unique(?),
    the Wild Cow of the Enclosure, Ninsun,
    your head is elevated over (other) men,
    Enlil has destined for you the kingship over the people."

[19 lines are missing here.]

Friends

129 They kissed each other and became friends.

[The Old Babylonian becomes fragmentary. The Standard Version resumes.]

145   "His strength is the mightiest in the land!
        His strength is as mighty as the meteorite(?) of Anu,
        . . ."
The mother of Gilgamesh spoke to *Gilgamesh*, saying;
Rimat-Ninsun said to *her son*:
    "(I ?), Rimat-Ninsun . . .
    My son . . .
    Plaintively . . .
        . . .
        . . ."

---

the men were making merry,
a *lusanu* (musical instrument) was set up,
for the man straightest(?) of feature,
for Gilgamesh, as for a god,
the *mehru* (antiphon?, counterpart?) was set up.
For Ishara the bed was ready,
Gilgamesh was to come together with the girls at night.

155 She went up into his (Shamash's) gateway,
    plaintively she implored . . . :
        "Enkidu has no father or mother,
        his shaggy hair no one cuts.
        He was born in the wilderness, no one raised him."
    Enkidu was standing there, and heard the speech.
    He . . . and sat down and wept,
    his eyes filled with tears,
    his arms felt limp, his strength weakened.
    They took each other by the hand,
    and . . . their hands like . . .
        . . .
167 Enkidu made a declaration to (Gilgamesh?).[5]

[32 lines are missing here.]

A Hero's Challenge

[Enkidu is speaking.]

200   "In order to protect the Cedar Forest
        Enlil assigned (Humbaba) as a terror to human beings—
        Humbaba's roar is a Flood, his mouth is Fire, and his breath
                                            is Death!
        He can hear 100 leagues away any rustling(?) in his forest!
        Who would go down into his forest?
        Enlil assigned him as a terror to human beings,
        and whoever goes down into his forest paralysis(?) will strike!"
    Gilgamesh spoke to Enkidu saying:

208   "What you say . . ."

[About 42 lines are missing here in the Standard Version; lines 228–49 are taken from the Old Babylonian.]

228   "Who, my Friend, can ascend to the heavens?[6]
        (Only) the gods can dwell forever with Shamash.

5. In the Old Babylonian Enkidu bemoans the loss of his physical strength: "My Friend, a groan chokes my throat, my arms are slack, and my strength has weakened." Gilgamesh proposes to journey to the Cedar Forest to kill the Guardian Humbaba and cut down the Cedar. Enkidu reacts with fear.
    6. Gilgamesh here recites proverbs on human mortality and expresses his desire to establish immortality through a great deed.

As for human beings, their days are numbered,
and whatever they keep trying to achieve is but wind!
Now you are afraid of death—
what has become of your bold strength?
I will go in front of you,
and *your* mouth can call out: 'Go on closer, do not be afraid!'
Should I fall, I will have established my fame.
(They will say:) 'It was *Gilgamesh* who locked in battle with
Humbaba the Terrible!'
You were born and raised in the wilderness,
a lion leaped up on you, so you have experienced it all![7]

[5 lines are fragmentary.]

I will undertake it and I will cut down the Cedar.
It is I who will establish fame for eternity!
Come, my friend, I will go over to the forge
and have them cast the weapons in our presence!"
249 Holding each other by the hand they went over to the forge.

[The Standard Version resumes at this point.]

250 The craftsmen sat and discussed with one another.
"We should fashion the axe . . .
The hatchet should be one talent in weight . . .
Their swords should be one talent . . .
Their armor one talent, their armor . . ."
Gilgamesh said to the men of Uruk:
"Listen to me, men . . .

[5 lines are missing here.]

262 "You, men of Uruk, who know . . .
I want to make myself more mighty, and will go on a *distant*(?)
journey!
I will face fighting such as I have never known,
I will set out on a road I have never traveled!
Give me your blessings! . . .
I will enter the city gate of Uruk . . .
I will devote(?) myself to the New Year's Festival.

7. The sense of this line is unclear.

I will perform the New Year's (ceremonies) in . . .
The New Year's Festival will take place, celebrations . . .
They will keep shouting 'Hurrah!' in . . ."[8]
272 Enkidu spoke to the Elders:
"What the men of Uruk . . .
Say to him that he must not go to the Cedar Forest—
the journey is not to be made!
A man who . . .
The Guardian of the Cedar Forest . . .
. . .
. . ."
280 The Noble Counselors of Uruk arose and
delivered their advice to Gilgamesh:
"You are young, Gilgamesh, your heart carries you off—
you do not know what you are talking about!
. . . gave birth to you.
Humbaba's roar is a Flood,
his mouth is Fire, his breath Death!
He can hear any rustling(?) in his forest 100 leagues away!
Who would go down into his forest?
Who among (even?) the Igigi gods can confront him?
In order to keep the Cedar safe, Enlil assigned him as a terror
to human beings."
291 Gilgamesh listened to the statement of his Noble Counselors.
[About 5 lines are missing to the end of Tablet II.]

8. The Old Babylonian version has Gilgamesh deliver a briefer but more comprehensible speech here.
Gilgamesh spoke the following to the Elders of Uruk-of-the-Plazas:
" . . . the god of whom they talk I would see!
He at whose name the lands are carried away I would conquer in the Cedar
Forest!
I will make the land hear how mighty is the Scion of Uruk!
I will set my hand to it and will chop down the Cedar,
I will establish for myself a Name for eternity!"

TABLET
III

The Elders reluctantly agree to the journey, but put the responsibility for the king's welfare on Enkidu, who is supposed to take the risky front position. They also stress the importance of friends helping each other. Distraught, Gilgamesh's mother, the goddess Ninsun, first criticizes the Sun God Shamash for having given Gilgamesh such "a restless heart," and then pleads with him to watch over the heroes during this perilous journey. She also charges Enkidu with the responsibility for Gilgamesh's safe return. They finally set out on their journey, trusting that Shamash will guide them. After a long break in the text, in a fragmentary passage Ninsun performs a ritual, seeming to initiate Enkidu into the cult of the female votaries of Ishtar—a most curious and intriguing notion. Following another long break, the Elders again commend Gilgamesh to Enkidu's care. In a panic Enkidu tries once again to dissuade Gilgamesh from the undertaking; the final lines of the tablet are lost, but clearly Gilgamesh remains confident of success, for the beginning of Tablet IV finds them on the journey.

This is one of the worst-preserved tablets of the Standard Version. The end of Old Babylonian Tablet III corresponds to the beginning of the Standard Version Tablet III, though the differences are considerable.

TABLET III

Precautions and Preparations

1 The Elders spoke to Gilgamesh, saying:
   "Gilgamesh, do not put your trust in (just) your vast strength,
   but keep a sharp eye out, make each blow strike its mark!
   'The one who goes on ahead saves the comrade.'[1]
   'The one who knows the route protects his friend.'
   Let Enkidu go ahead of you;
   he knows the road to the Cedar Forest,
   he has seen fighting, has experienced battle.
   Enkidu will protect the friend, will keep the comrade safe.
   Let his body urge him back to the wives (?)."
   [The Elders speak to Enkidu:]
   "In our Assembly we have entrusted the King to you (Enkidu),
   and on your return you must entrust the King back to us!"
13 Gilgamesh spoke to Enkidu, saying:
   "Come on, my friend, let us go to the Egalmah Temple,
   to Ninsun, the Great Queen;
   Ninsun is wise, all-knowing.
   She will put the advisable path at our feet."
   Taking each other by the hand,
20 Gilgamesh and Enkidu walked to the Egalmah ("Great Palace"),
   to Ninsun, the Great Queen.
   Gilgamesh arose and went to her.
   "Ninsun, (even though) *I am extraordinarily* strong (?) . . .
   I must now travel a long way to where Humbaba is,
   I must face fighting such as I have not known,
   and I must travel on a road that I do not know!
   Until the time that I go and return,

1. Proverbial sayings.

until I reach the Cedar Forest,
until I kill Humbaba the Terrible,
and eradicate from the land something baneful that Shamash
hates,
intercede with Shamash on my behalf! (?)
[The placement of the following fragment of five lines is inexact.]
If I kill Humbaba and cut his Cedar(?)
let there be *rejoicing all over the land* (?),
and I will erect a monument of the victory (?) before you!"

A Mother's Prayers

35 *The . . . words* of Gilgamesh, her son,
grieving (?) Queen Ninsun heard over and over.
Ninsun went into her living quarters.
She washed herself with the purity plant,
she donned a robe worthy of her body,
she donned jewels worthy of her chest,
she donned her sash, and put on her crown.
She sprinkled water from a bowl onto the ground.
She . . . and went up to the roof.
She went up to *the roof* and set incense in front of Shamash,
45 she offered fragrant cuttings, and raised her arms to Shamash.
"Why have you imposed—nay, inflicted!—a restless heart on
my son, Gilgamesh?
Now you have touched him so that he wants to travel
a long way to where Humbaba is!
He will face fighting such as he has not known,
and will travel on a road that he does not know!
Until he goes away and returns,
until he reaches the Cedar Forest,
until he kills Humbaba the Terrible,
and eradicates from the land something baneful that you hate,
on the day that you see him on the road(?)
may Aja, the Bride, without fear remind you,

and command also the Watchmen of the Night,
58 *the stars,* and at night *your father, Sin.*"
[The next 90-odd lines are fragmentary or missing.]

The Sacred Bond

150 She (Ninsun) banked up the incense and uttered the ritual words.²
She called to Enkidu and would give him instructions:
"Enkidu the Mighty, you are not of my womb,
but now I speak to you along with the sacred votaries of
                                                 Gilgamesh,
the high priestesses, the holy women, the temple servers."
She laid a pendant(?) on Enkidu's neck,
the high-priestesses took . . .
and the "daughters-of-the-gods" . . .
"I have taken . . . Enkidu . . .
Enkidu to . . . Gilgamesh *I have taken.*"

. . .

. . .

"Until he goes and returns,
until he reaches the Cedar Forest,
be it a month . . .
165 be it a year . . ."
[About 11 lines are missing here, and the placement of the following fragment is uncertain.]
177 . . . the gate of cedar . . .
Enkidu . . . in the Temple of *Shamash,*
(and) Gilgamesh in the Egalmah.
He made an offering of cuttings . . .
. . . the sons of the *king*(?) . . .
[Perhaps some 60 lines are missing here.³]

2. The next line is very obscure but may allude to Enkidu's initiation into a cult of female votaries of Gilgamesh.
3. The Old Babylonian contains a long string of cautions by the Elders to Gilgamesh, including warnings against Humbaba's clever stratagems, and instructions to wash his feet in Humbaba's river, to dig a well at each stopover so that there will be fresh water for offerings to Shamash, and to be mindful of Lugalbanda (his father, who also traveled over distant mountains).

The Final Blessings

[The Elders reluctantly commend Gilgamesh to the protection of Enkidu.]

242   "Enkidu will protect the friend, will keep the comrade safe.
Let his body urge him back to the wives (?).
In our Assembly we have entrusted the King to you,
and on your return you must entrust the King back to us!"
Enkidu spoke to Gilgamesh saying:
"My Friend, turn back! . . .⁴
The road . . ."

[The last 10–20 lines are missing.]

4. The Old Babylonian ending differs: Enkidu exhorts Gilgamesh to set out, to have no fear, but to look to Enkidu for safety. Gilgamesh's reply is lost; the men then say: "May you achieve your goal!"

TABLET
IV

On each stage of the six days' journey to the Cedar Forest (to the northwest) Gilgamesh performs offerings to his protector Shamash, asking for a favorable message from him. Shamash sends his message through fearful and ominous dreams, which Enkidu interprets, however, in a positive light. The last dream is not preserved, and what follows is highly uncertain. With the fragments as placed in this translation, Gilgamesh seems finally to be afraid, and reminds Shamash of his promise to Ninsun to protect him. Shamash indicates that it is the time to enter the forest, for Humbaba has taken off his protective garments. Enkidu and Gilgamesh have a fight because Enkidu has lost his courage and threatens to turn back. Humbaba hears the sound of their fighting, is enraged at the intruders, and probably challenges them (there is a break in the text here). Gilgamesh manages to convince Enkidu that in unity there is strength and safety, and they stand together ready to go into the forest.

Large passages of this tablet are missing, but there is enough evidence that the same camp ritual was repeated at each stage to warrant full restoration. One missing dream is supplied from an Old Babylonian tablet. The understanding of the last two columns (line 225 to end) is extremely tentative, and good arguments have been made for placing the fragment in Tablet V, with the necessary adjustments to interpretation.

TABLET IV

The Journey To The Cedar Forest
FIRST STAGE

1 At twenty leagues they broke for some food,
at thirty leagues they stopped for the night,
walking fifty leagues in a whole day,
a walk of a month and a half.
On the third day they drew near to the Lebanon.
They dug a well facing Shamash (the setting sun),
. . .
Gilgamesh climbed up a mountain peak,
made a libation of flour, and said:
10   "Mountain, bring me a dream, a favorable message from
                                 Shamash."
Enkidu prepared *a sleeping place for him* for the night;
a violent wind passed through so he attached *a covering*.
He made him lie down, and . . . in a circle.
They . . . like grain from the mountain . . .
While Gilgamesh rested his chin on his knees,
sleep that pours over mankind overtook him.
17 In the middle of the night his sleep came to an end,
so he got up and said to his friend:
     "My friend, did you not call out to me? Why did I wake up?
     Did you not touch me? Why am I so disturbed?
     Did a god pass by? Why are my muscles trembling?
     Enkidu, my friend, I have had a dream—
     and the dream I had was deeply disturbing!
24   In the mountain gorges . . .
     the mountain fell down on me (us ?) . . .
     We(?) . . . like flies(?) . . ."
He who was born in the wilderness,

Enkidu, interpreted the dream for his friend:
    "My friend, your dream is favorable.
    The dream is extremely important . . .
    My friend, the mountain which you saw in the dream is
                            Humbaba.
    (It means) we will capture Humbaba, and kill him
    and throw his corpse into the wasteland.
    In the morning there will be a favorable message from Shamash."

SECOND STAGE

35 At twenty leagues they broke for some food,
at thirty leagues they stopped for the night,
walking fifty leagues in a whole day,
a walk of a month and a half.
They dug a well facing Shamash

. . .

Gilgamesh climbed up a mountain peak,
made a libation of flour, and said:
43   "Mountain, bring me a dream, a favorable message from
                            Shamash."
Enkidu prepared *a sleeping place for him* for the night;
a violent wind passed through so he attached *a covering*.
He made him lie down, and . . . in a circle.
They . . . like grain from the mountain . . .
While Gilgamesh rested his chin on his knees,
sleep that pours over mankind overtook him.
50 In the middle of the night his sleep came to an end,
so he got up and said to his friend:
    "My friend, did you not call out to me? Why did I wake up?
    Did you not touch me? Why am I so disturbed?
    Did a god pass by? Why are my muscles trembling?
    Enkidu, my friend, I have had a dream,
    besides my first dream (I have had) a second.
    And the dream I had—so striking, so . . . , so disturbing![1]

1. The dream given here as the second dream is actually from an Old Babylonian fragment.

58   I was grappling with a wild bull of the wilderness,
      with his bellow he *split* the ground, a cloud of dust . . . to
                                                              the sky.
      I sank to my knees in front of him.
      He holds . . . that encircled(?) my arm.
      (My?) tongue(?) hung out(?) . . .
      My temples throbbed(?) . . .
      He gave me water to drink from his waterskin."

[Enkidu interprets the dream:]

65   "My friend, the god to whom we go
      is not the wild bull! He is totally different!
      The wild bull that you saw is Shamash, the protector,
      in difficulties he holds our hand.
      The one who gave you water to drink from his waterskin
      is your (personal) god, who brings honor to you, Lugalbanda.
      We should join together and do one thing,
      a deed such as has never (before) been done *in the land*."

                    THIRD STAGE

73 At twenty leagues they broke for some food,
    at thirty leagues they stopped for the night,
    walking fifty leagues in a whole day,
    a walk of a month and a half.
    They dug a well facing Shamash,
    . . .
    Gilgamesh climbed up a mountain peak,
    made a libation of flour, and said:
81   "Mountain, bring me a dream, a favorable message from
                                                          Shamash."
    Enkidu prepared *a sleeping place for him* for the night;
    a violent wind passed through so he attached *a covering*.
    He made him lie down, and . . . in a circle.
    They . . . like grain from the mountain . . .
    While Gilgamesh rested his chin on his knees,
    sleep that pours over mankind overtook him.

88 In the middle of the night his sleep came to an end,
so he got up and said to his friend:
"My friend, did you not call out to me? Why did I wake up?
Did you not touch me? Why am I so disturbed?
Did a god pass by? Why are my muscles trembling?
Enkidu, my friend, I have had a third dream,
and the dream I had was deeply disturbing.
95 The heavens roared and the earth rumbled;
(then) it became deathly still, and darkness loomed.
A bolt of lightning cracked and a fire broke out,
and where(?) it kept thickening, there rained death.
Then the white-hot flame dimmed, and the fire went out,
and everything that had been falling around turned to ash.
Let us go down into the plain so we can talk it over."
102 Enkidu heard the dream that he had presented and said to Gilgamesh:

[About 40 lines are missing here, containing the interpretation and possibly another stage of the journey.]

FOURTH STAGE

143 At twenty leagues they broke for some food,
at thirty leagues they stopped for the night,
walking fifty leagues in a whole day,
a walk of a month and a half.
They dug a well facing Shamash,
. . .
Gilgamesh climbed up a mountain peak,
made a libation of flour, and said:
151 "Mountain, bring me a dream, a favorable message from
Shamash."
Enkidu prepared *a sleeping place for him* for the night;
a violent wind passed through so he attached *a covering*.
He made him lie down, and . . . in a circle.
They . . . like grain from the mountain . . .
While Gilgamesh rested his chin on his knees,
sleep that pours over mankind overtook him.

158 In the middle of the night his sleep came to an end,
so he got up and said to his friend:
"My friend, did you not call out to me? Why did I wake up?
Did you not touch me? Why am I so disturbed?
Did a god pass by? Why are my muscles trembling?
Enkidu, my friend, I have had a *fourth*(?) dream,
and the dream I had was deeply disturbing (?).
[About 5 lines are missing.]
170   "He was . . . cubits tall . . .

     . . .

     . . . Gilgamesh . . ."
[Several lines are missing.]
Enkidu listened to his dream . . .
177   "The dream that you had is favorable, it is extremely important!
My friend, this . . .
Humbaba like . . .
Before it becomes light . . .
We will achieve (victory?) over him,
Humbaba, against whom we rage,
we will . . . and triumph over him.
In the morning there will be a favorable message from Shamash."

FIFTH   STAGE

185 At twenty leagues they broke for some food,
at thirty leagues they stopped for the night,
walking fifty leagues in a whole day,
a walk of a month and a half.
They dug a well facing Shamash,

. . .

Gilgamesh climbed up a mountain peak,
made a libation of flour, and said:
193   "Mountain, bring me a dream, a favorable message from
                                        Shamash."
Enkidu prepared *a sleeping place for him* for the night;
a violent wind passed through so he attached *a covering*.

He made him lie down, and . . . in a circle.
They . . . like grain from the mountain . . .
While Gilgamesh rested his chin on his knees,
sleep that pours over mankind overtook him.
200 In the middle of the night his sleep came to an end,
so he got up and said to his friend:
     "My friend, did you not call out to me? Why did I wake up?
     Did you not touch me? Why am I so disturbed?
     Did a god pass by? Why are my muscles trembling?
     Enkidu, my friend, I had a fifth(?) dream,
206   and the dream I had was deeply disturbing (?).
[The lines containing the dream are fragmentary or missing. The remaining lines may
or may not belong to the end of Tablet IV.²]

United They Stand

225 His tears were running in the presence of Shamash.
     "What you said in Uruk . . . ,
     be mindful of it, stand by me . . . !"
Gilgamesh, the offspring of Uruk-*Haven,*
Shamash heard what issued from *his* mouth,
and suddenly there resounded a warning sound from the sky.
     "Hurry, stand by him so that he (Humbaba) does not *enter
                                                     the forest,*
     and does not go down into the thickets *and hide* (?)!
     He has not put on his seven coats of armor(?),³
     he is wearing only one, but has taken off six."
235 They (Gilgamesh and Enkidu ?) . . .
They lunge at each other like raging wild bulls . . .
One time he bellowed full of . . .

2. What happens after the dreams is still unclear because there is no consensus on
the correct position of fragment K.8591. It could be understood as the last two columns
of Tablet IV (as presented also in this translation, with diffidence), but good arguments
have been made for its belonging to the first two columns of Tablet V! Although several
lines of K.8591 correspond to lines in a Hittite fragment, the adjacent lines are so differ-
ent that the Hittite cannot be used as a guide.
    3. The Akkadian says clearly "seven cloaks," but the Old Babylonian mentions the
"seven terrors." The mention of the cloaks/terrors here derives from the Sumerian epic
tale "Gilgamesh and Huwawa," where the encounter is developed much differently.

The Guardian of the Forest bellowed . . .

239 Humbaba like . . .

[22 lines are missing until this fragment resumes with line 262. A fragment of another tablet belongs somewhere in the gap.[4] Gilgamesh speaks to Enkidu:]

"'One alone cannot . . .'

'Strangers . . .'

'A slippery path is not feared by two people who help each
other.'

'Twice three times . . .'

'A three-ply rope *cannot be cut*.'

'The mighty lion—two cubs *can roll him over*.'"

[Some lines may be missing before the next fragment resumes.]

262 *Enkidu* spoke to *Gilgamesh, saying*:

"*As soon as we* have gone down *into the Cedar Forest,*

let us split open the tree (?) and strip off *its branches* (?)."

Gilgamesh spoke to *Enkidu,* saying:

"Why, my friend, we . . . so wretchedly (?) . . .

We have crossed over all *the mountains* together,

. . . in front of us, before we have cut down *the Cedar*.

My friend, you who are so experienced in battle,

who . . . fighting,

you . . .[5] and (need) not fear *death*.

. . .

273 Let your *voice* bellow forth like the kettledrum,

let the stiffness in your arms depart,

let the paralysis in *your legs* go away.

Take my hand, my friend, we will go on together.

Your heart should burn to do battle

—pay no heed to death, do not *lose heart*!

4. It appears that Enkidu has lost his courage, which Gilgamesh tries to bolster with old sayings that in unity there is strength and safety. The Sumerian epic "Gilgamesh and Humbaba" contains some vaguely similar sayings. The three-ply rope as a metaphor for the strength and safety of friends together has a close parallel in Ecclesiastes 4:9–12. See the discussion in Tigay, *Evolution*, pp. 165–77.

5. The verb is completely preserved but can be analyzed as a form of *sabatu*, "to sweep (with the hand), to wave back and forth," or *lapatu*, "to touch (oneself), to smear over (oneself)." Some scholars thus suggest a restoration and interpretation "Since you have smeared yourself with (magical) plants you need not fear *death*."

The one who watches from the side is a careful man,
but the one who walks in front protects himself and saves his
comrade,
and through their fighting they establish fame!"
As the two of them reached the *evergreen forest*
285 they cut off their talk, and stood still.

TABLET
V

The Cedar Forest was luxurious and bountiful, a primeval forest, with a path leading straight in; the friends apparently began cutting trees. Alerted by the sound of falling trees, Humbaba confronts the pair and seems (the text is extremely fragmentary) to warn them off. Enkidu in turn warns that the two of them can overpower the single Humbaba. Humbaba tells Gilgamesh, whom he apparently knows and respects, that a noble of his sort should not be led by the "nobody" Enkidu. The intensity of the vilification suggests that Humbaba has had some prior knowledge of Enkidu, too, leading to his present hostility. Contorting his monstrous face, Humbaba utters dire threats that send Gilgamesh into hiding. Enkidu stirs up Gilgamesh's failed courage, and they engage in a mighty struggle with Humbaba. The friends prevail only through the intervention of the Sun God Shamash. At sword's point Humbaba begs Gilgamesh for his life and offers to provide him with all the trees he wants and to become his servant. Gilgamesh is indecisive, but Enkidu presses him to kill Humbaba before the gods discover them, so that Gilgamesh will achieve fame as the slayer of Humbaba. The deed is done, but not before Humbaba utters a final ominous curse. Not satisfied with ordinary trees, Enkidu determines to cut down the tallest cedar, which he intends to fashion into a door for the Temple of Enlil at Nippur. They make a raft of the trees and sail down the Euphrates with Gilgamesh holding the head of Humbaba.

The important encounter with Humbaba in the Cedar Forest was among the worst-preserved tablets of the Gilgamesh Epic. In 1980, however, an incomplete tablet from Uruk itself (Late Babylonian period) was published, providing much more of the episode. Though it fills in much missing material, it also raises the question of how "standard" our Standard Version is, for this Late Babylonian Tablet V begins at a point corresponding to about line 80 of the Neo-Assyrian Tablet V. It is possible that in Uruk a rather different version of the Epic existed, at least in the distribution of text over the tablets. The Old Babylonian fragments have substantially different versions of the encounter; the Hittite-language fragments have some parallels to the Standard Version and are used for occasional restoration.

TABLET V

The Cedar Forest

[The first lines are from the Neo-Assyrian.]

1 They stood at the forest's edge,
gazing at the top of the Cedar Tree,
gazing at the entrance to the forest.
Where Humbaba would walk there was a trail,
the roads led straight on, the path was excellent.
Then they saw the Cedar Mountain, the Dwelling of the Gods, the
                                                throne dais of Irnini.
Across the face of the mountain the Cedar brought forth luxurious
                                                                foliage,
its shade was good, extremely pleasant.
The thornbushes were matted together, the woods(?) were a thicket
. . . among the Cedars, . . . the boxwood,
the Forest was surrounded by a ravine two leagues long,
12 . . . and again for two-thirds (of that distance),

[35 lines are missing in the Neo-Assyrian.]

48 Suddenly the swords . . . ,
and after the sheaths . . . ,
the axes were smeared . . .
dagger and sword . . .
alone . . .

. . .

Humbaba *spoke to Gilgamesh(?) saying*:
    "He does not *come* (?) . . .

[8 lines are missing from the Neo-Assyrian.]

64   Enlil . . ."
Enkidu spoke to Humbaba, saying: [1]

---

1. These lines repeat the proverbial sayings about strength in unity as in Tablet IV. Enkidu here tries to warn Humbaba that he has no chance against the combined strength of the two friends.

"Humbaba . . .
'One alone . . .'
'*Strangers* . . .'
'A slippery path is not feared by two people who help each other.'
'Twice three times . . .'
'A three-ply rope *cannot be cut.*'
72   'The mighty lion—two cubs *can roll him over.*'"

[The entire rest of the Neo-Assyrian tablet is missing; after a small break the beginning of the Late Babylonian tablet seems to continue the tale.]

75 Humbaba spoke to Gilgamesh, saying: [2]

"An idiot [3] and a moron should give advice to each other,
but you, Gilgamesh, why have you come to me?
Give advice, Enkidu, you 'son of a fish,' who does not even
know his own father,
to the large and small turtles which do not suck their moth-
er's milk!
When you were still young I saw you but did not go over to you;
. . . you, . . . in my belly.
. . . , you have brought Gilgamesh into my presence,
. . . you stand . . . an enemy, a stranger.
. . . Gilgamesh, throat and neck,
I would feed your flesh to the screeching vulture, the eagle, and
the vulture!"

The Capture of Humbaba

86 Gilgamesh spoke to Enkidu, saying:
"My Friend, Humbaba's face keeps changing! [4]
. . .
. . ."

90 Enkidu spoke to Gilgamesh, saying: [5]

2. Humbaba's diatribe with animal metaphors is deeply obscure, but may in some way play on the proverbs earlier quoted. Note that Humbaba addresses himself to (master) Gilgamesh, though the speech seems actually directed to Enkidu.
3. The word *lillu* means both "idiot" and "(a kind of demon)"; Gilgamesh was, according to the Sumerian King List, the son of a *lillu* demon.
4. Or, is "strange, different."
5. Gilgamesh was apparently so frightened by how ferocious Humbaba's face had turned that he ran away and hid. Enkidu here tries to shore up Gilgamesh's courage in

"Why, my friend, are you whining so pitiably,
hiding behind your whimpering?
Now there, my friend, . . .
in the coppersmith's channel . . . ,
again to blow (the bellows?) for an hour, the glowing (metal)(?)
　　　　　　　　　　　　　　　　　　　. . . for an hour.
To send the Flood, to crack the Whip.[6]
Do not snatch your feet away, do not turn your back,
98　　. . . strike even harder!"

[20–25 lines are missing here.]

120　. . . may they be expelled.
. . . distant.
. . . head fell . . . and it/he confronted him . . .
The ground split open with the heels of their feet,
as they whirled around in circles Mt. Hermon and Lebanon split.
The white clouds darkened,
death rained down on them like fog.
Shamash raised up against Humbaba mighty tempests[7]—

---

the face of Humbaba, reminding him how carefully the smiths had prepared their weapons (?) (end of Tablet III).

6. Names of mythical weapons, also mentioned in the Sumerian epic.

7. A long Hittite fragment gives a very different version of the events preceding the sending of the winds.

He (Enkidu) seized the axe in his hand . . . ,
. . . but when Gilgamesh . . .
then this one seized the axe . . . and felled the cedar.
But when Humbaba heard the commotion he became enraged (saying:)
　　"Who has come and desecrated the trees,
　　my mountain . . . , and has felled the Cedar?"
Then from the sky the heavenly Shamash spoke to them (Gilgamesh and Enkidu):
　　"Go on in, fear not, as long as he (Humbaba) does not return.
　　. . ."
Hearing this Enkidu became angry,
Enkidu and Gilgamesh entered (the forest),
stirring up the anger of Humbaba in the middle of the mountain.
He said to them:
　　"I shall carry you off and cast you down from the sky,
　　smash you on the *head*(?) and drive you down into the dark earth!"
He carried them off but did not cast them down from the sky,
on the *head*(?) he smashed them but did not drive them into the dark earth.
[Several lines are fragmentary.]
He (Gilgamesh) entered the . . . of the heavenly Shamash,
his tears flowing in streams, and said to heavenly Shamash:

Southwind, Northwind, Eastwind, Westwind, Whistling Wind,
Piercing Wind, Blizzard, Bad Wind, Wind of Simurru,
Demon Wind, Ice Wind, Storm, Sandstorm—
thirteen winds rose up against him and covered Humbaba's face.
He could not butt through the front, and could not scramble out
the back,
so that Gilgamesh's weapons were in reach of Humbaba.
134 Humbaba begged for his life, saying to Gilgamesh:
"You are young yet, Gilgamesh, your mother gave birth to you,
and you are the offspring of *Rimat-Ninsun* (?) . . .
(It was) at the word (= instigation) of Shamash, Lord of the
Mountain,
that you were roused (to this expedition).
O scion of the heart of Uruk, King Gilgamesh!
. . . Gilgamesh . . .

. . .

Gilgamesh, *let me go* (?),
I will dwell with you *as your servant*(?).[8]
As many trees as you command me *I will cut down for you*,
I will guard for you myrtle wood . . . ,
wood fine enough *for your palace*!"
146 Enkidu addressed Gilgamesh, saying:
"My friend, do not listen to Humbaba,

[20 lines are missing. Apparently Humbaba sees that Gilgamesh is influenced by En-
kidu, and tries to dissuade Enkidu.]

168 "You understand the rules of my forest, the rules . . . ,
further, you are aware of all the things 'So ordered (by Enlil).'[9]

" . . . same day that in the city . . .
because he had settled again in the city . . .
So I set out for the heavenly Shamash,
have made the journey . . ."
[The sending of the winds follows directly.]
    8. The ends of the lines here are restored based on the Hittite, which reads "You will
be my master, I will be your servant. I will fell for you the trees, . . . , *I will build* houses
for you from it."
    9. The sense is that Enkidu was always aware of the special protective status of
Humbaba and the forest (Tablet III), and that·he should bear in mind that there will
surely be severe divine consequences.

I should have carried you up, and killed you at the very en-
trance to the branches of my forest.
I should have fed your flesh to the screeching vulture, the eagle,
and the vulture.
So now, Enkidu, clemency is up to you.
Speak to Gilgamesh to spare (my) life!"
174 Enkidu addressed Gilgamesh, saying:
My friend, Humbaba, Guardian of the Cedar Forest,
grind up, kill, pulverize(?), and . . . him!
Humbaba, Guardian of the Forest, grind up, kill, pulverize(?),
and . . . him!
Before the Preeminent God Enlil hears . . .
and the . . . gods be filled with rage against us.
Enlil is in Nippur, Shamash is in Sippar.
Erect an eternal monument proclaiming . . .
how Gilgamesh killed(?) Humbaba."
183 When Humbaba heard . . .
. . . Humbaba

[About 50 lines are missing, recounting probably the final struggle and capture of
Humbaba, resuming with his last demand that Enkidu intercede with Gilgamesh.]

235   . . . the forest.
and denunciations(?) have been made.
But you are sitting there like a shepherd . . .
and like a 'hireling of his mouth.'
Now, Enkidu, clemency is up to you.
Speak to Gilgamesh that he spare (my) life!"
Enkidu spoke to Gilgamesh, saying:
"My friend, Humbaba, Guardian of the Forest,
grind up, kill, pulverize(?), and . . . him!
Before the Preeminent God Enlil hears,
and the . . . gods are full of rage at us.
Enlil is in Nippur, Shamash is in Sippar.
Erect an eternal monument proclaiming . . .
how Gilgamesh killed(?) Humbaba."

The Curse and the Killing

249 Humbaba heard . . .

[About 30 lines are missing. Humbaba realizes there is no hope, and utters a curse portending Enkidu's early death.]

280 "May he not live the longer of the two,
may Enkidu not have any 'shore'(?) more than his friend
Gilgamesh!"

Enkidu spoke to Gilgamesh, saying:
"My friend, I have been talking to you but you have not been
listening to me,[10]
You have been listening to the curse *of Humbaba!*"
. . .
. . . his friend
. . . by his side
. . .
. . . they pulled out his insides including his tongue.
. . . he jumped(?).
. . .
. . . abundance fell over the mountain.
293 . . . abundance fell over the mountain.

[30 lines are missing.]

The Cedar

324 They cut through the Cedar,
. . .
While Gilgamesh cuts down the trees, Enkidu searches through
the *urmazallu.*
Enkidu addressed Gilgamesh, saying:
"My friend, we have cut down the towering Cedar whose top
scrapes the sky.
Make from it a door 72 cubits high, 24 cubits wide,

10. Gilgamesh is now having second thoughts because of the curse, but Enkidu again insists on the killing.

one cubit thick, its fixture, its lower and upper pivots will be
out of one piece.
Let them carry it to Nippur, the Euphrates will carry it down,
Nippur *will rejoice* (?).
. . ."
They tied together a raft . . .
Enkidu *steered it* . . .
344 while Gilgamesh *held* the head of Humbaba.

TABLET
VI

B ack in Uruk, and restored to his regal finery, Gilgamesh attracts the eye of Ishtar, goddess of love. She proposes marriage, sweetening the proposal with offers of power and wealth. He rejects her, contemptuously listing the miseries she has caused her previous lovers (in reference to other myths). With the fury of a woman scorned, she convinces her father, Anu, to send the Bull of Heaven to attack Uruk, in spite of the devastation it will bring to the land and people. After the Bull causes hundreds of the men of Uruk to fall into chasms in the earth, Enkidu and Gilgamesh dispatch it in a classic scenario of bullfighting. As Ishtar rages, Enkidu savagely shouts he would do the same to her, and hurls the Bull's thigh into her face. That night, as Ishtar and her cult women mourn the Bull, Gilgamesh, Enkidu, and the men celebrate their triumph.

This is the shortest tablet of the epic, and one of the most complete. Although the Sumerian Epic "Gilgamesh and the Bull of Heaven" was known in the Old Babylonian period, it was probably not integrated into the Old Babylonian Epic of Gilgamesh, where the killing of Humbaba was sufficient motivation for punishing Enkidu. Allusions to the Bull of Heaven do appear in fragments of the Middle Babylonian Epic.

TABLET VI

A Woman Scorned

1 He washed out his matted hair and cleaned up his equipment(?),
shaking out his locks down over his back,
throwing off his dirty clothes and putting on clean ones.
He wrapped himself in regal garments and fastened the sash.
When Gilgamesh placed his crown on his head,
6 Princess Ishtar raised her eyes to the beauty of Gilgamesh.
 "Come along, Gilgamesh, be you my husband,
 to me grant your lusciousness.[1]
 Be you my husband, and I will be your wife.
 I will have harnessed for you a chariot of lapis lazuli and gold,
 with wheels of gold and 'horns' of electrum(?).
 It will be harnessed with great storming mountain mules!
 Come into our house, with the fragrance of cedar.
 And when you come into our house the doorpost(?) and throne
 dais(?)[2] will kiss your feet.
 Bowed down beneath you will be kings, lords, and princes.
 The Lullubu people[3] will bring you the produce of the moun-
 tains and countryside as tribute.
 Your she-goats will bear triplets, your ewes twins,
 your donkey under burden will overtake the mule,
 your steed at the chariot will be bristling to gallop,
 your ox at the yoke will have no match."
21 Gilgamesh addressed Princess Ishtar saying:
 "What would I have to give you if I married you?

1. Literally "fruit."
2. Instead of "doorposts and throne dais" possibly "most excellent purification priests."
3. The Lullubu were a wild mountain people living in the area of modern-day western Iran. The meaning is that even the wildest, least controllable of peoples will recognize Gilgamesh's rule and bring tribute.

Do you need oil or garments for your body?
Do you lack anything for food or drink?
I would gladly feed you food fit for a god,
I would gladly give you wine fit for a king,
. . .
. . . may the street(?) be your home(?),
. . . may you be clothed in a garment,
and may any lusting man (?) marry you!
You are an oven who . . . ice,
a half-door that keeps out neither breeze nor blast,
a palace that crushes down valiant warriors,
an elephant who devours its own covering,
pitch that blackens the hands of its bearer,
a waterskin that soaks its bearer through,
limestone that buckles out the stone wall,
a battering ram that attracts the enemy land,
a shoe that bites its owner's feet!
40   Where are your bridegrooms that you keep forever?
Where is your 'Little Shepherd' bird *that went up over you*?
See here now, I will recite the list of your lovers.
Of the shoulder (?) . . . his hand,
Tammuz, the lover of your earliest youth,
for him you have ordained lamentations year upon year!
You loved the colorful 'Little Shepherd' bird
and then hit him, breaking his wing, so
now he stands in the forest crying 'My Wing'!
49   You loved the supremely mighty lion,
yet you dug for him seven and again seven pits.
You loved the stallion, famed in battle,
yet you ordained for him the whip, the goad, and the lash,
ordained for him to gallop for seven and seven hours,
ordained for him drinking from muddied waters,[4]
you ordained for his mother Silili to wail continually.
You loved the Shepherd, the Master Herder,

4. Horses put their front feet in the water when drinking, churning up mud.

who continually presented you with bread baked in embers,
and who daily slaughtered for you a kid.
Yet you struck him, and turned him into a wolf,
so his own shepherds now chase him
and his own dogs snap at his shins.

62 You loved Ishullanu, your father's date gardener,
who continually brought you baskets of dates,
and brightened your table daily.
You raised your eyes to him, and you went to him:
    'Oh my Ishullanu, let us taste of your strength,
    stretch out your hand to me, and touch our "vulva."' [5]
Ishullanu said to you:
    'Me? What is it you want from me?
    Has my mother not baked, and have I not eaten
    that I should now eat food under contempt and curses
    and that alfalfa grass should be my only cover against
                                    the cold?'
As you listened to these his words
you struck him, turning him into a dwarf(?), [6]
and made him live in the middle of his (garden of) labors,
where the *mihhu* do not go up, nor the bucket of dates (?) down.
And now me! It is me you love, and you will ordain for me as
                                    for them!"

Her Fury

78 When Ishtar heard this
in a fury she went up to the heavens,
going to Anu, her father, and crying,
going to Antum, her mother, and weeping:
    "Father, Gilgamesh has insulted me over and over,
    Gilgamesh has recounted despicable deeds about me,
    despicable deeds and curses!"

---

5. This line probably contains a word play on *hurdatu* as "vulva" and "date palm," the latter being said (in another unrelated text) to be "like the vulva."
    6. Or "frog"?

Anu addressed Princess Ishtar, saying:
"What is the matter? Was it not you who provoked King
Gilgamesh?
So Gilgamesh recounted despicable deeds about you,
despicable deeds and curses!"
89 Ishtar spoke to her father, Anu, saying:
"Father, give me the Bull of Heaven,
so he can kill Gilgamesh in his dwelling.
If you do not give me the Bull of Heaven,
I will knock down the Gates of the Netherworld,
I will smash the door posts, and leave the doors flat down,
and will let the dead go up to eat the living!
And the dead will outnumber the living!"
Anu addressed Princess Ishtar, saying:
"If you demand the Bull of Heaven from me,
there will be seven years of empty husks for the land of Uruk.
Have you collected grain for the people?
Have you made grasses grow for the animals?"
Ishtar addressed Anu, her father, saying:
"I have heaped grain in the granaries for the people,
I made grasses grow for the animals,
in order that they might eat in the seven years of empty husks.
I have collected grain for the people,
I have made grasses grow for the animals."
[About 6 lines are missing here.]
114 When Anu heard her words,
he placed the nose-rope of the Bull of Heaven in her hand.
Ishtar led the Bull of Heaven down to the earth.
When it reached Uruk

. . .

It climbed down to the Euphrates . . .
At the snort of the Bull of Heaven a huge pit opened up,
and 100 Young Men of Uruk fell in.
At his second snort a huge pit opened up,
and 200 Young Men of Uruk fell in.

At his third snort a huge pit opened up,
and Enkidu fell in up to his waist.
Then Enkidu jumped out and seized the Bull of Heaven by its horns.
The Bull spewed his spittle in front of him,
with his thick tail he flung *his dung behind him* (?).
129 Enkidu addressed Gilgamesh, saying:
"My friend, we can be bold(?) . . .
How shall we respond . . .
My friend, I saw . . .
And my strength . . .
I will rip out . . .
I and you, we must share (?)
I shall grasp the Bull
I will fill *my hands* (?) . . .
In front . . .
. . .
Between the nape, the horns, and . . . thrust your sword."
141 Enkidu stalked and *hunted down* the Bull of Heaven.
He grasped it by the thick of its tail
and held onto it with both his hands (?),
while Gilgamesh, like an *expert butcher*,
boldly and *surely approached the Bull of Heaven*.
Between the nape, the horns, and . . . he thrust his sword.
After they had killed the Bull of Heaven,
they ripped out its heart and presented it to Shamash.
They withdrew, bowing down humbly to Shamash.
Then the brothers sat down together.
151 Ishtar went up onto the top of the Wall of Uruk-Haven,
cast herself into the pose of mourning, and hurled her woeful curse:
"Woe unto Gilgamesh who slandered me and killed the Bull of
Heaven!"
When Enkidu heard this pronouncement of Ishtar,
he wrenched off the Bull's hindquarter and flung it in her face:
"If I could only get at you I would do the same to you!
I would drape his innards over your arms!"

158 Ishtar assembled the (cultic women) of lovely-locks, joy-girls, and
                                                                harlots,
and set them to mourning over the hindquarter of the Bull.
Gilgamesh summoned all the artisans and craftsmen.
(All) the artisans admired the thickness of its horns,
each fashioned from 30 minas of lapis lazuli!
Two fingers thick is their casing(?).
Six vats of oil the contents of the two
he gave as ointment to his (personal) god Lugalbanda.
He brought the horns in and hung them in the bedroom of the family
                                        head (Lugalbanda?).
They washed their hands in the Euphrates,
and proceeded hand in hand,
striding through the streets of Uruk.
The men of Uruk gathered together, staring at them.
171 Gilgamesh said to the palace retainers:
    "Who is the bravest of the men?
    Who is the boldest of the males?
    —Gilgamesh is the bravest of the men,
    the boldest of the males!
    She at whom we flung the hindquarter of the Bull of Heaven in
                                                                anger,
    Ishtar has no one that pleases her . . . in the street (?)
    . . ."
177 Gilgamesh held a celebration in his palace.
The Young Men dozed off, sleeping on the couches of the night.
Enkidu was sleeping, and had a dream.
182 He woke up and revealed his dream to his friend.

TABLET
VII

Through the medium of a dream, Enkidu learns that he has been singled out for punishment. The chief gods in council decide that the killing of Humbaba and the Bull of Heaven, and the cutting of the Cedar, must be punished, but Enlil insists that it be only Enkidu who dies. Frantic at the injustice of his impending doom, Enkidu curses the Cedar Door—it is for cutting the Cedar that the gods have condemned him. Gilgamesh seems to chastise his blasphemy, promising a memorial statue to him and finest honors. Enkidu then vindictively appeals to the god Shamash to ruin the trapper and the harlot because they are the ones ultimately responsible for bringing him out of his wild and morally neutral state into the turbulent world of emotions and choice and responsibility. Shamash, however, reminds him of the truly human happiness he has known through the harlot who brought him to Gilgamesh. Shamash counsels him to be grateful for the good he did enjoy, and for the deep sense of loss that will be felt on his death. Falling sick, Enkidu confides in Gilgamesh another awful dream: a monstrous demon attacked him, and Gilgamesh did not even try to save him; the demon carried Enkidu off into the Netherworld, the bleak House of Dust (Decay), full of the once-famous. A long passage about the Netherworld is missing at this point. Enkidu's condition deteriorates over 12 days, and with his last breath he seems to accuse Gilgamesh of abandoning him.

The text of this tablet is not well preserved in the Standard Version, and has been supplemented by several tablets of the Middle Babylonian period from Mesopotamia as well as from Hittite Anatolia and Canaan. A Middle Babylonian fragment in Akkadian from ancient Megiddo is apparently from a tablet containing selected excerpts of the text; its chief importance is in showing that Mesopotamian literature was known in Canaan in the fourteenth century B.C.

TABLET VII

Protestations of Innocence

[The first line is taken from the catch-line at the end of Tablet VI; the next 25 lines are taken from a Hittite fragment.]

1   "My friend, why are the Great Gods in conference?
   (In my dream) Anu, Enlil, and Shamash held a council,
   and Anu spoke to Enlil:
    'Because they killed the Bull of Heaven and have also slain
                    Humbaba,
    the one of them who pulled up the Cedar of the Mountain
                    must die!'
   Enlil said: 'Let Enkidu die, but Gilgamesh must not die!'
   But the Sun God of Heaven[1] replied to valiant Enlil:
    'Was it not at my[2] command that they killed the Bull of
               Heaven and Humbaba?
   Should now *innocent* Enkidu die?'
10   Then Enlil became angry at Shamash, saying:
    '(It is you who are responsible ?) because you traveled daily
         with them as their friend!'"
Enkidu was lying (sick) in front of Gilgamesh.
His tears flowing like canals, he (Gilgamesh) said:
   "O brother, dear brother, why are they absolving me instead of
             my brother?"
Then (Enkidu said:) "So now must I become a ghost,
   to sit with the ghosts of the dead, to see my dear brother
             nevermore?"

[The Hittite breaks; perhaps a fragment from Megiddo belongs in the gap.]

Enkidu . . . , said to *Enlil*(?):

---

1. The Hittite name of Shamash.
2. The text has "your," probably a scribal error for "my." Nowhere in the Epic is Enlil said to be responsible for instigating these deeds. Shamash prompted Gilgamesh to go to the Cedar Forest.

"I did not cut down the *Cedar*,

. . .

. . .

In the Cedar Forest *where the Great Gods* dwell,
I did *not* kill *the Cedar*."
[The Standard Version resumes.]
23 Enkidu addressed Gilgamesh,
saying to Gilgamesh, his Friend:
    "Come, Friend, . . .

    . . .

    The door . . ."
[4 lines are missing here.]

The Door of Cedar Cursed

32 Enkidu raised his eyes, . . .
and spoke to the door as if it were human:
    "You stupid wooden door,
    with no ability to understand . . . !
    Already at 20 leagues I selected the wood for you,
    until I saw the towering Cedar . . .
    Your wood was without compare *in my eyes*.
    Seventy-two cubits was your height, 24 cubits your width, one
                                cubit your thickness,
    your door post, pivot stone, and post cap . . .
    I fashioned you, and I carried you; to Nippur . . .
    Had I known, O door, that this would be *your gratitude*
    and this your gratitude . . . ,
    I would have taken an axe and chopped you up,
    and lashed *your planks* into a raft!

    . . .

48   In its gate I erected the . . .

    . . .

    and in Uruk . . .
    . . . they heard . . .
    But yet, O door, I fashioned you, and I carried you to Nippur!

May a king who comes after me reject you,
may the god . . .
may he remove my name and set his own name there!"
He ripped out . . . threw down.
57 He (Gilgamesh) kept listening to his words, and retorted quickly,
Gilgamesh listened to the words of Enkidu, his Friend, and his tears
flowed.
Gilgamesh addressed Enkidu, saying:
"*Friend, the gods have given you* a mind[3] broad and . . .
Though it behooves you to be sensible, *you keep uttering
improper things!*
Why, my Friend, does your mind utter improper things?
The dream is important but very frightening,
your lips are buzzing like flies.
Though there is much fear, the dream is very important.
To the living they (the gods) leave sorrow,
to the living the dream leaves pain.
I will pray, and beseech the Great Gods,
I will seek . . . , and appeal to your god.
70 . . . Enlil, the Father of the Gods,
. . . Enlil the Counselor . . . you.
I will fashion a statue of you of gold without measure,
do not worry . . . , gold . . .
What Enlil says is not . . .
What he has said cannot go back, cannot . . . ,
What . . . he has laid down cannot go back, cannot . . .
My friend, . . . of fate goes to mankind."

The Trapper Cursed

78 Just as dawn began to glow,
Enkidu raised his head and cried out to Shamash,
at the (first) gleam of the sun his tears poured forth.
"I appeal to you, O Shamash, on behalf of my precious life (?),
because of that notorious trapper

3. The word means "heart, insides, interior" and by extension "mind, feelings."

who did not let me attain the same as my friend (*ibru*).
May the trapper not get enough to feed himself (*epru*).
May his profit be slashed, and his wages decrease,
may . . . be his share before you,
may he not enter . . . but go out of it like vapor(?)!"[4]

The Harlot Cursed

88 After he had cursed the trapper to his satisfaction,
his heart prompted him to curse the Harlot.

"Come now, Harlot, I am going to decree your fate,
a fate that will never come to an end for eternity!
I will curse you with a Great Curse,
may my curses overwhelm you suddenly, in an instant!
May you not be able to make a household,
and not be able to love a child of your own (?)!
May you not dwell in the . . . of girls,
may dregs of beer (?) stain your beautiful lap,
may a drunk soil your festal robe with vomit(?),
. . . the beautiful (?)
. . . of the potter.

101 May you never acquire anything of bright alabaster,
may the judge . . .
may shining silver(?), man's delight, not be cast into your house,
may a gateway be where you take your pleasure,[5]
may a crossroad be your home,
may a wasteland be your sleeping place,
may the shadow of the city wall be your place to stand,
may the thorns and briars skin your feet,
may both the drunk and the dry slap you on the cheek,
. . . in your city's streets (?),
. . .
may the lion(?) roar at you . . .

113 may the builder not seal the roof of your house,

4. Or "out through a window!"
5. Or "be your birthing room."

may owls nest in the cracks of your walls!
may no parties take place . . .
. . .
. . . present(?).
. . .
and your filthy "lap" . . . may . . . be his(?) gift!
Because of me . . .
while I, blameless, you have . . . against me."

The Harlot Blessed

122 When Shamash heard what his mouth had uttered,
he suddenly called out to him from the sky:
"Enkidu, why are you cursing the harlot, Shamhat,
she who fed you bread fit for a god,
she who gave you wine fit for a king,
she who dressed you in grand garments,
and she who allowed you to make beautiful Gilgamesh your
comrade?
Now Gilgamesh is your beloved brother-friend!
He will have you lie on a grand couch,
will have you lie on a couch of honor.
He will seat you[6] in the seat of ease, the seat at his left,
so that the princes of the world kiss your feet.
He will have the people of Uruk go into mourning and moaning
over you,
will fill the happy people with woe over you.
And after you[7] he will let his body bear a filthy mat of hair,
will don the skin of a lion and roam the wilderness."
138 As soon as Enkidu heard the words of valiant Shamash,
his agitated heart grew calm, his anger abated.
Enkidu spoke to the harlot, saying:
"Come, Shamhat, I will decree your fate for you.
Let my mouth which has cursed you, now turn to bless you!

6. That is, "the statue of you."
7. That is, "after your death."

May governors and nobles love you,
May he who is one league away bite his lip (in anticipation
of you),
may he who is two leagues away shake out his locks (in
preparation)!
May the soldier not refuse you, but undo his buckle for you,
may he give you rock crystal(?), lapis lazuli, and gold,
may his gift to you be earrings of filigree(?).
May . . . his supplies be heaped up.
May he bring you into the . . . of the gods.
May the wife, the mother of seven (children), be abandoned
because of you!"

A Dream of the Dead

152 Enkidu's innards were churning,
lying there so alone.
He spoke everything he felt, saying to his friend:
   "Listen, my friend, to the dream that I had last night.
   The heavens cried out and the earth replied,
   and I was standing between them.
   There appeared a man of dark visage—
   his face resembled the Anzu,[8]
   his hands were the paws of a lion,
   his nails the talons of an eagle!—
   he seized me by my hair and overpowered me.
   I struck him a blow, but he skipped about like a jump rope,
   and then he struck me and capsized me like a *raft*,
   and trampled on me like a wild bull.
   He encircled my whole body in a clamp.
167   'Help me, my friend!' (I cried),
   but you did not rescue me, you were afraid and did not . . ."
   [4 lines are missing here.]
173   "Then he . . . and turned me into a dove,
   so that my arms *were feathered* like a bird.

---

8. The lion-headed eagle of mythology.

Seizing me, he led me down to the House of Darkness, the
dwelling of Irkalla,
to the House where those who enter do not come out,
along the road of no return,
to the House where those who dwell do without light,
where dirt is their drink, their food is of clay,
where, like a bird, they wear garments of feathers,
and light cannot be seen, they dwell in the dark,
and upon the door and bolt lies dust.
On entering the House of Dust,
everywhere I looked there were royal crowns gathered in heaps,
everywhere I listened, it was the bearers of crowns who in the
past had ruled the land,
but who now served Anu and Enlil cooked meats,
served confections, and poured cool water from waterskins.

188 In the House of Dust that I entered
there sat the high priest and acolyte,
there sat the purification priest and ecstatic,
there sat the anointed priests of the Great Gods.
There sat Etana, there sat Sumukan,
there sat Ereshkigal, the Queen of the Netherworld.
Beletseri, the Scribe of the Netherworld, knelt before her,
she was holding the tablet[9] and was reading it out to her
(Ereshkigal).
She raised her head and when she saw me—

197 'Who has taken this *man*?' "

[Only the last word of a few of the next 50 lines remain: grave, Ereshkigal, ecstatic
priest, flood, Egalmah. The text resumes apparently with Enkidu speaking to
Gilgamesh:]

248 " . . . I(?) who went through every difficulty,
remember *me and forget (?) not* all that I went through
(with you)."

[Gilgamesh speaks:]
"My friend has had a dream that *bodes ill*(?)."

9. "The tablet" refers to the "Tablet of Destinies," inscribed with the fates of
the dead.

The day he had the dream . . . came to an end.

The Death of Enkidu

252 Enkidu lies down a first day, a second day,
that Enkidu . . . in his bed;
a third day and fourth day, that *Enkidu . . . in his bed*;
a fifth, a sixth, and seventh, *that Enkidu . . . in his bed*;
an eighth, a ninth, a tenth, *that Enkidu . . . in his bed.*
Enkidu's illness *grew ever worse.*
The eleventh and twelfth day *his illness grew ever worse.*
Enkidu *drew up* from his bed,
and called out to Gilgamesh . . . : [10]
261   "My friend hates me . . .
        (Once), while he *talked with me* in *Uruk*
        as I was afraid of the battle (with Humbaba), he encouraged me.
        My friend who *saved* me in battle *has now abandoned me*!
        I and *you* . . ."

[About 20 lines are missing here to the end of the tablet, telling of Enkidu's death. A passage from the Megiddo tablet may belong here.]

At his noises (death rattle) *Gilgamesh* was roused . . .
Like a dove he moaned . . .
        "May he not be held, in death . . .
        O preeminent among *men* . . ."
To his friend . . .
        "I will mourn him (?) . . .
        I at *his side* . . ."

---

10. Only the first half of the following lines are preserved, for which a totally different restoration and interpretation are found in A. Schott and Wolfram von Soden, *Das Gilgamesch-Epos* (Stuttgart: Philipp Reclam, 1958, rev. ed. 1982), p. 70:
        "I have been cursed, my friend, *with a great curse*,
        I do not die like one who *falls in fighting*,
        I was afraid of battle, *so I die without peace.*
        My friend, he who dies in battle *is fortunate.*
        But I *suffer disgrace in death* (?)."

TABLET
VIII

Watching by Enkidu's deathbed, Gilgamesh pours out a torrent of memories about their experiences together, and in disbelief touches the stilled heart. He then casts off his regal finery and puts on the rough skins of a wanderer of the wilderness. He has a rich memorial statue crafted, dedicated to "My Friend," as promised, and has the city go into mourning. Following a long break which probably involves funerary rituals, Gilgamesh makes an offering to Shamash, and then probably sets out on a journey. An earlier Sumerian work known as "The Lamentation over Enkidu" is too poorly preserved to compare to Tablet VIII. The Neo-Assyrian composition purporting to be a letter of Gilgamesh (discussed in the last section of the Introduction) draws on the material of this tablet.

Tablet VIII is very poorly preserved, missing more than 175 lines, and one of the principal texts is a school copy full of errors.

TABLET VIII

Lamentation over Enkidu

1 Just as day began to dawn
Gilgamesh addressed his friend, saying:
"Enkidu, your mother, the gazelle,
and your father, the wild donkey, engendered you,
four wild asses raised you on their milk,
and the herds taught you all the grazing lands.
May the Roads of Enkidu to the Cedar Forest mourn you
and not fall silent night or day.
May the Elders of the broad city of Uruk-Haven mourn you.
May the peoples who gave their blessing after us mourn you.
May the men of the mountains and hills mourn you.
May the . . .
May the pasture lands shriek in mourning as if it were your
mother.
May the . . . , the cypress, and the cedar which we destroyed(?)
in our anger mourn you.
15 May the bear, hyena, panther, tiger, water buffalo(?), jackal,
lion, wild bull, stag, ibex, all the creatures of the plains
mourn you.
May the holy River Ulaja, along whose banks we grandly used
to stroll, mourn you.
May the pure Euphrates, to which we would libate water from
our waterskins, mourn you.
May the men of Uruk-Haven, whom we saw in our battle when
we killed the Bull of Heaven, mourn you.
May the farmer . . . , who extols your name in his sweet work
song, mourn you.
May the . . . of the broad city, who . . . exalted your name,
mourn you.

May the herder . . . , who prepared butter and light beer for
your mouth, mourn you.
May . . . , who put ointments on your back, mourn you.
May . . . , who prepared fine beer for your mouth, mourn you.
24   May the harlot, . . . you rubbed yourself with oil and felt good,
mourn you.
May . . . , . . . of the wife placed(?) a ring on you . . . ,
mourn you.
. . .
May the brothers go into mourning over you like sisters;
. . . the lamentation priests, may their hair be shorn off on
your behalf.
Enkidu, your mother and your father are in the wastelands,
30   I mourn you . . .”

"Hear me, O Elders of Uruk, hear me, O men!
I mourn for Enkidu, my friend,
I shriek in anguish like a mourner.
You, axe at my side, so trusty at my hand—
you, sword at my waist, shield in front of me,
you, my festal garment, a sash over my loins—
an *evil demon*(?) appeared and took him away from me!
My friend, the swift mule, fleet wild ass of the mountain, pan-
ther of the wilderness,
Enkidu, my friend, the swift mule, fleet wild ass of the moun-
tain, panther of the wilderness,
after we joined together and went up into the mountain,
fought the Bull of Heaven and killed it,
and overwhelmed Humbaba, who lived in the Cedar Forest,
now what is this sleep which has seized you?
You have turned dark and do not hear me!"
45 But his (Enkidu's) eyes do not move,
he touched his heart, but it beat no longer.
He covered his friend's face like a bride,
swooping down over him like an eagle,

and like a lioness deprived of her cubs
he keeps pacing to and fro.
He shears off his curls and heaps them onto the ground,
ripping off his finery and casting it away as an abomination.

The Monument to "My Friend"

53 Just as day began to dawn, Gilgamesh . . .
and issued a call to the land:
> "You, blacksmith! You, lapidary! You, coppersmith!
> You, goldsmith! You, jeweler!
> Create 'My Friend,' *fashion a statue of him.*
> . . . he fashioned a statue of his friend.
> His features . . .
> . . . , your chest will be of lapis lazuli, your skin will be of gold."

[20 lines are missing here.[1]]

81 > "I had you recline on the great couch,
> indeed, on the couch of honor I let you recline,
> I had you sit in the position of ease, the seat at the left, so the
> > princes of the world kissed your feet.
> I had the people of Uruk mourn and moan for you,
> I filled happy people with woe over you,
> and after you (died) I let a filthy mat of hair grow over my body,
> and donned the skin of a lion and roamed the wilderness."

Just as day began to dawn,
he undid his straps . . .
91 . . . carnelian,

[85 lines are missing here.[2]]

177 > " . . . to my friend.
> . . . your dagger

1. In the break was probably a description of Gilgamesh sitting in ritual mourning
for six days and seven nights, since this is mentioned in Tablet X.
2. Another tablet fragment with the ends of some twenty lines on each side may be-
long here in the Epic of Gilgamesh or may be a related text. It mentions jewels, precious
stones, gold "for his friend," gold overlays, followed by some offerings of "*mashaltappu*
of the earth/Netherworld" to Shamash, and the phrases "may he go by his side,"
"whose forehead is of lapis lazuli," "inlaid with carnelian."

. . .
to Bibbi . . ."

[40 lines are missing here.]

221 " . . . the judge of the Anunnaki."
When Gilgamesh heard this
the *zikru* of the river(?) he created[3] . . .
Just as day began to dawn Gilgamesh opened(?) . . .
and brought out a big table of sissoo wood.
A carnelian bowl he filled with honey,
a lapis lazuli bowl he filled with butter.
228 He provided . . . and displayed it before Shamash.

[All of the last column, some 40–50 lines, is missing.]

3. See notes 4 and 9 to Tablet I for the difficulty with the meaning of *zikru*.

TABLET
IX

Gilgamesh is grief-stricken by the loss of his friend, and becomes acutely aware that such will one day be his own fate. Rebelling, he determines to find the secret of eternal life from the only mortal man known to have attained it. This is Utanapishtim, a king who in ancient times survived the great Flood, and now lives at the Mouth of the Rivers, at the end of the earth. In spite of what the surviving fragments suggest is an ominous dream, Gilgamesh sets out. On the first stage of his quest he meets a scorpion-being and its mate, who guard the passage through the mountain of the rising sun. They try to dissuade him from this treacherous and ultimately futile journey, but Gilgamesh insists and they allow him on. Through ten leagues of pitch darkness (the hours of deep night) he walks, until at dawn, the twelfth hour, he finds himself in a fabulous jeweled garden. He continues on to the edge of the sea, where he sees the house of Siduri.

This is the worst-preserved tablet of the entire Standard Version, and may have been composed relatively late in the development of the Epic. A Hittite fragment of the Middle Babylonian period has a parallel to the curious episode of the attack by two lions at night and the appeal to the Moon God Sin (IX, 7–9), followed immediately (3 lines later) by the departure of Gilgamesh and his reaching the sea where Siduri lived.

TABLET IX

The Quest

1 Over his friend, Enkidu, Gilgamesh cried bitterly, roaming the
                                       wilderness.
    "I am going to die!—am I not like Enkidu?!
    Deep sadness penetrates my core,
    I fear death, and now roam the wilderness—
    I will set out to the region of Utanapishtim, son of Ubartutu,
                        and will go with utmost dispatch!
    When I arrived at mountain passes at nightfall,[1]
    I saw lions, and I was terrified!
    I raised my head in prayer to Sin,
    to . . . *the Great Lady* of the gods my supplications poured
                      forth, 'Save me from . . . !'"
  He was sleeping *in the night,* but awoke with a start with a dream:
11 *A warrior*(?) enjoyed his life—
    he raised his axe in his hand,
    drew the dagger from his sheath,
    and fell into their midst like an arrow.
    He struck . . . and he scattered *them,*
    . . .

    . . .

    . . .

    The name of the former . . .
    The name of the second . . .
  [26 lines are missing here, telling of the beginning of his quest.]

    1. The tenses in the next lines are difficult, and have been "adjusted" for sense. This enigmatic episode with the killing of two lions is referred to again in Tablet X, 57, and parallels. The Hittite fragment reads: "The heroic god Sin *said*: 'These two lions which you have killed, go take the two of them into the city, take them into the temple of Sin.'" Both the lion and the following dream episode seem garbled.

The Scorpion-Beings

47 The mountain is called Mashu.
When he reached Mount Mashu,
which daily guards the rising and setting of the Sun,
above which only the dome of the heavens reaches,
and whose flank reaches as far as the Netherworld below,
there were Scorpion-beings watching over its gate.
Trembling terror they inspire, the sight of them is death,
their frightening aura sweeps over the mountains.
At the rising and setting they watch over the Sun.
When Gilgamesh saw them, trembling terror blanketed his face,
but he pulled himself together and drew near to them.

58 The scorpion-being called out to his female:
"He who comes to us, his body is the flesh of gods!"
The scorpion-being, his female, answered him:
"(Only) two-thirds of him is a god, one-third is human."
The male scorpion-being called out,
saying to the offspring of the gods:
"*Why have you traveled* so distant a journey?
Why have you come here to me,
over rivers whose crossing is treacherous?
I want to learn your . . .
. . .
69 I want to learn . . ."

[26 lines are missing here. When the text resumes Gilgamesh is speaking.]

136 "I have come on account of my ancestor Utanapishtim,
who joined the Assembly of the Gods, and *was given eternal life*.
About Death and Life *I must ask him!*"
The scorpion-being spoke to Gilgamesh . . . , saying:
"Never has there been, Gilgamesh, *a mortal man who could
do that*(?).
No one has crossed through the mountains,
for twelve leagues it is darkness throughout—
dense is the darkness, and light there is none.

To the rising of the sun . . .
To the setting of the sun . . .
To the setting of the sun . . .
They caused to go out . . ."

[67 lines are missing, in which Gilgamesh convinces the scorpion-being to allow him passage.]

215   "Though it be in deep sadness *and pain,*
in cold or heat . . .
gasping after breath . . . *I will go on!*
Now! *Open the Gate!*"
The scorpion-being spoke to Gilgamesh, saying:
"Go on, Gilgamesh, *fear not!*
The Mashu mountains *I give to you freely* (?),
the mountains, the ranges, *you may traverse* . . .
In safety may *your feet carry you.*
The gate of the mountain . . ."

The Journey Through the Night

225 As soon as Gilgamesh heard this
he heeded the utterances of the scorpion-being.
Along the Road of the Sun[2] he journeyed—
one league *he traveled* . . . ,
dense was the darkness, light there was none.
Neither *what lies ahead nor* behind does it allow him *to see.*

2. The Road of the Sun refers to the course of the sun through the Netherworld at night. There seem to be some vague echoes of Gilgamesh's journey on the Road of the Sun in an Old Babylonian tablet, though the rest of that tablet parallels Tablet X of the Standard Version.
Shamash was agitated and leaned down to him, saying to Gilgamesh:
"Gilgamesh, where are you roving?
Life that you are seeking you will not find!"
Gilgamesh spoke to valiant Shamash saying:
"Since my wandering and roaming all over the wilderness,
is there enough resting in the ground (?)?
I will sleep there all the (remaining) years.
May my eyes behold the sun that I may be saturated with light.
Is the darkness far off—how much light is there?
When could the dead ever see the rays of the sun?
[The text breaks.]

Two leagues *he traveled* . . . ,
dense was the darkness, light there was none,
233 neither *what lies ahead nor* behind does it allow him *to see.*

[22 lines are missing here; the missing third stage must have had a considerable embellishment to account for these lines.]

256 Four leagues *he traveled* . . . ,
dense was the darkness, light there was none,
neither *what lies ahead nor* behind does it allow him *to see.*
Five leagues *he traveled* . . . ,
dense was the darkness, light there was none,
neither *what lies ahead nor* behind does it allow him *to see.*
Six leagues *he traveled* . . . ,
dense was the darkness, light there was none,
neither *what lies ahead nor* behind does it allow him *to see.*
Seven leagues *he traveled* . . . ,
dense was the darkness, light there was none,
neither *what lies ahead nor* behind does it allow him *to see.*
268 Eight leagues *he traveled* and cried out (?),
dense was the darkness, light there was none,
neither *what lies ahead nor* behind does it allow him *to see.*
Nine leagues *he traveled* . . . the North Wind.
It licked at his face,
dense was the darkness, light there was none,
neither *what lies ahead nor* behind does it allow him *to see.*
Ten leagues he traveled . . .
. . . is near,
. . . four leagues.
Eleven leagues he traveled and came out before the sun(rise).
Twelve leagues he traveled and it grew brilliant.

The Jeweled Garden

280 *Before him there were* trees of precious stones,
and he went straight to look at them.
The tree bears carnelian as its fruit,
laden with clusters (of jewels), dazzling to behold,

—it bears lapis lazuli as foliage,
bearing fruit, a delight to look upon.

[25 lines are missing here, describing the garden in detail.]

311 . . . cedar
. . . agate[3]
. . . of the sea . . . lapis lazuli,
like thorns and briars . . . carnelian,
. . . , . . . jasper
rubies, hematite, . . .

. . .

like . . . emeralds (?)
. . . of the sea,

. . .

Gilgamesh . . . on walking onward,
322 raised his eyes *and saw* . . .

3. Some stone names cannot be identified with the modern stones; the words translated "agate, rubies, emeralds" are the English literary clichés for a jeweled garden.

TABLET

X

Gilgamesh comes upon the tavern-keeper Siduri, who lives by the sea. Seeing his haggard appearance and thinking he is a murderer, she locks herself in. Gilgamesh pounds on the door, insisting that he is indeed the famous Gilgamesh, brought to this sorry state by grief and fear. He demands directions to Utanapishtim. Siduri protests that his journey is impossible, that no one can cross the sea with its Waters of Death. She nonetheless points out Urshanabi, the ferryman of Utanapishtim, who might take him across. His approach to Urshanabi is as belligerent as to Siduri—he attacks and destroys certain critical "stone things" of Urshanabi's boat. Identifying himself as before, Gilgamesh demands directions to Utanapishtim. The ferryman protests that Gilgamesh has himself ruined the crossing by destroying the "stone things" of the boat. He then has Gilgamesh cut some punting poles to push the boat, so his hands will not come in contact with the Waters of Death. After a long voyage Gilgamesh meets a man, and again explains how he has come to his present condition and why he must go on to find Utanapishtim. The man—actually Utanapishtim, whom Gilgamesh does not recognize—counsels Gilgamesh that death is a fact of life because the gods have so decreed, and that all human endeavors are by nature transient.

Although only about half of Tablet X is preserved, so much is repetition that long fragmentary passages can be safely restored. There are still a number of difficulties in understanding some passages, but this is due to uncertainty in the reading of the cuneiform or to the obscurity of its thought (e.g., lines 258ff.) rather than to poor preservation. An Old Babylonian fragment has parallels to several of the episodes, and reveals how the older version differs in style and content. Some of the parallel Old Babylonian passages are quoted in notes. A Hittite fragment also preserves the encounter with Urshanabi.

TABLET X

The Tavern-Keeper by the Sea

1 The tavern-keeper Siduri who lives by the seashore,
she lives . . .
the pot-stand was made for her, the golden fermenting vat was made
                                                        for her.
She is covered with a veil . . .
Gilgamesh was roving about . . .
wearing a skin, . . .
having the flesh of the gods in his body,
but sadness deep within him,
looking like one who has been traveling a long distance.
The tavern-keeper was gazing off into the distance,
puzzling to herself, she said,
wondering to herself:
    "That fellow is surely a *murderer*(?)!
    Where is he heading? . . ."
As soon as the tavern-keeper saw him, she bolted her door,
bolted her gate, bolted the lock.
17 But at her noise Gilgamesh pricked up his ears,
lifted his chin (to look about) and then laid his eyes on her.
Gilgamesh spoke to the tavern-keeper, saying:
    "Tavern-keeper, what have you seen that made you bolt
                                                    your door,
    bolt your gate, bolt the lock?
    If you do not let me in I will break your door, and smash
                                                    the lock!
    . . .
    . . . the wilderness."
 . . . Gilgamesh
 . . . gate

. . .

. . .

Gilgamesh said to the tavern-keeper:

"*I am Gilgamesh*, I killed the Guardian!

I destroyed Humbaba who lived in the Cedar Forest,

I slew lions in the mountain passes!

I grappled with the Bull that came down from heaven, and

killed him."

34 The tavern-keeper spoke to Gilgamesh, saying:

"*If you are Gilgamesh*, who killed the Guardian,

who destroyed Humbaba who lived in the Cedar Forest,

who slew lions in the mountain passes,

who grappled with the Bull that came down from heaven, and

killed him,

why are your cheeks emaciated, your expression desolate?

Why is your heart so wretched, your features so haggard?

Why is there such sadness deep within you?

Why do you look like one who has been traveling a long

distance

so that ice and heat have seared your face?

. . . you roam the wilderness?"

45 Gilgamesh spoke to her, to the tavern-keeper he said:

"Tavern-keeper, should not my cheeks be emaciated?

Should my heart not be wretched, my features not haggard?

Should there not be sadness deep within me?

Should I not look like one who has been traveling a long

distance,

and should ice and heat not have seared my face?

. . . , should I not roam the wilderness?

My friend, the wild ass who chased the wild donkey, panther of

the wilderness,

Enkidu, the wild ass who chased the wild donkey, panther of

the wilderness,

we joined together, and went up into the mountain.

We grappled with and killed the Bull of Heaven,

we destroyed Humbaba who lived in the Cedar Forest,
we slew lions in the mountain passes!

My friend, whom I love deeply, who went through every hard-
ship with me,
Enkidu, whom I love deeply, who went through every hardship
with me,
the fate of mankind has overtaken him.
Six days and seven nights I mourned over him
and would not allow him to be buried
until a maggot fell out of his nose.
I was terrified *by his appearance*(?),
I began to fear death, and so roam the wilderness.
The issue of my friend oppresses me,
so I have been roaming long trails through the wilderness.
The issue of Enkidu, my friend, oppresses me,
so I have been roaming long roads through the wilderness.
How can I stay silent, how can I be still?
My friend whom I love has turned to clay.
Am I not like him? Will I lie down, never to get up again?"[1]

1. In the Standard Version Gilgamesh's outpouring is entirely rhetorical, since
he does not wait for a response from the tavern-keeper but demands directions to
Utanapishtim. In the Old Babylonian version, however, the tavern-keeper offers her in-
sights on the true goal of life, which is not to escape death, but to enjoy the normal, if
transitory, pleasures of life.
"Gilgamesh, where are you wandering?
The life that you are seeking all around you will not find.
When the gods created mankind
they fixed Death for mankind,
and held back Life in their own hands.
Now you, Gilgamesh, let your belly be full!
Be happy day and night,
of each day make a party,
dance in circles day and night!
Let your clothes be sparkling clean,
let your head be clean, wash yourself with water!
Attend to the little one who holds onto your hand,
let a wife delight in your embrace.
This is the (true) task of *mankind*(?)."
(Some restore the last words differently, as "this is the task of *womankind*," and take it
to refer to intercourse as the natural duty of women, as it was for the harlot in Tablet I.)
    This advice seems to be similar to some (fragmentary) lines in a Sumerian composi-
tion that mentions Ziusudra (= Utanapishtim), which suggests that the ideas are part

73 Gilgamesh spoke to the tavern-keeper, saying:
    "So now, tavern-keeper, what is the way to Utanapishtim?
    What are its markers? Give them to me! Give me the markers!
    If possible, I will cross the sea;
    if not, I will roam through the wilderness."
The tavern-keeper spoke to Gilgamesh, saying:
    "There has never been, Gilgamesh, any passage whatever,
    there has never been anyone since days of yore who crossed
                                                    the sea.
    The (only) one who crosses the sea is valiant Shamash, except
                                                    for him who can cross?
    The crossing is difficult, its ways are treacherous—
    and in between are the Waters of Death that bar its approaches!
    And even if, Gilgamesh, you should cross the sea,
    when you reach the Waters of Death what would you do?
    Gilgamesh, over there is Urshanabi, the ferryman of Utanapishtim.
    'The stone things'[2] are with him, he is in the woods picking
                                                    mint(?).
    Go on, let him see your face.
    If possible, cross with him;
    if not, you should turn back."

The Ferryman

91 When Gilgamesh heard this
    he raised the axe in his hand,
    drew the dagger from his belt,
    and slipped stealthily away after them.
    Like an arrow he fell among them ("the stone things").
    From the middle of the woods their noise could be heard.

_____

of traditional Mesopotamian wisdom, shifted by the Old Babylonian author to another
character.
    2. The nature of the mysterious "stone things" (literally, "those of stone") has been
much discussed in the literature, and they are often assumed to be some protective
amulets or images. New analysis of an important early Sumerian myth suggests, how-
ever, that the "stone things" are a mythological allusion whose meaning is still ex-
tremely obscure.

Urshanabi, the sharp-eyed, saw . . .
When he heard the axe, he ran toward it.
He struck his head . . . Gilgamesh.[3]
He clapped his hands and . . . his chest,
while "the stone things" . . . the boat
. . . Waters of Death
. . . broad sea
in the Waters of Death . . .
. . . to the river
. . . the boat
. . . on the shore.
Gilgamesh spoke to Urshanabi (?), the ferryman,
      " . . .
      . . . you."

111 Urshanabi spoke to Gilgamesh, saying:[4]
      "Why are your cheeks emaciated, your expression desolate?
      Why is your heart so wretched, your features so haggard?
      Why is there such sadness deep within you?
      Why do you look like one who has been traveling a long
                                                    distance
      so that ice and heat have seared your face?
      Why . . . you roam the wilderness?"
Gilgamesh spoke to Urshanabi, saying:
      "Urshanabi, should not my cheeks be emaciated, my expression
                                                    desolate?
      Should my heart not be wretched, my features not haggard?
      Should there not be sadness deep within me?
      Should I not look like one who has been traveling a long
                                                    distance,

3. The beginnings and ends of the next several lines are taken from tablets of differ-
ent cities and centuries, and may not be matched correctly.
4. What follows in the Standard Version is a word-for-word repetition of the ex-
change with the tavern-keeper. The Old Babylonian version of lines ca. 109–52 is differ-
ent and much shorter. Urshanabi asks Gilgamesh his name; Gilgamesh replies "I am
Gilgamesh who came from Uruk, the House of Anu, who wended through the moun-
tains, the long road of the rising sun." He then demands to be shown Utanapishtim the
Faraway. The first three lines of the response are missing but it seems that Urshanabi
then agrees to take Gilgamesh by boat. The two then "had a discussion."

and should ice and heat not have seared my face?
. . . should I not roam the wilderness?
My friend who chased wild asses in the mountain, the panther
of the wilderness,
Enkidu, my friend, who chased wild asses in the mountain, the
panther of the wilderness,
we joined together, and went up into the mountain.
We grappled with and killed the Bull of Heaven,
we destroyed Humbaba who dwelled in the Cedar Forest,
we slew lions in the mountain passes!
My friend, whom I love deeply, who went through every hard-
ship with me,
Enkidu, my friend, whom I love deeply, who went through
every hardship with me,
the fate of mankind has overtaken him.
134   Six days and seven nights I mourned over him
and would not allow him to be buried
until a maggot fell out of his nose.
I was terrified *by his appearance*(?),
I began to fear death, and so roam the wilderness.
The issue of my friend oppresses me,
so I have been roaming long trails through the wilderness.
The issue of Enkidu, my friend, oppresses me,
so I have been roaming long roads through the wilderness.
How can I stay silent, how can I be still?
My friend whom I love has turned to clay;
Enkidu, my friend whom I love, has turned to clay!
Am I not like him? Will I lie down, never to get up again?"
147 Gilgamesh spoke to Urshanabi, saying:
"Now, Urshanabi! What is the way to Utanapishtim?
What are its markers? Give them to me! Give me the markers!
If possible, I will cross the sea;
if not, I will roam through the wilderness!"

The Waters of Death

152 Urshanabi spoke to Gilgamesh, saying:
   "It is your hands, Gilgamesh, that prevent the crossing!
   You have smashed 'the stone things,' you have pulled out their
                                                    retaining ropes (?).
   'The stone things' have been smashed, their retaining ropes (?)
                                                    pulled out!
   Gilgamesh, take the axe in your hand, go down into the woods,
   and cut down 300 punting poles each 60 cubits in length.
   Strip them, attach caps(?), and bring them to the boat!"
   When Gilgamesh heard this
   he took up the axe in his hand, drew the dagger from his belt,
   and went down into the woods,
   and cut 300 punting poles each 60 cubits in length.
   He stripped them and attached caps(?), and brought them to
                                                    the boat.
164 Gilgamesh and Urshanabi boarded the boat,
   Gilgamesh launched the *magillu*-boat[5] and they sailed away.
   By the third day they had traveled a stretch of a month and a
                                                    half, and
   Urshanabi arrived at the Waters of Death.
   Urshanabi said to Gilgamesh:
      "Hold back, Gilgamesh, *take a punting pole*,
      but your hand must not pass over the Waters of Death . . . !
      Take a second, Gilgamesh, a third, and a fourth pole,
      take a fifth, Gilgamesh, a sixth, and a seventh pole,
      take an eighth, Gilgamesh, a ninth, and a tenth pole,
      take an eleventh, Gilgamesh, and a twelfth pole!"
   In twice 60 rods Gilgamesh had used up the punting poles.
   Then he loosened his waist-cloth(?) for . . .
   Gilgamesh stripped off his garment
   and held it up on the mast(?) with his arms.

   5. *Magillu* is the name of a boat taken from mythology. It appears in the same early
Sumerian myth that refers to the "stone things."

Utanapishtim

179 Utanapishtim was gazing off into the distance,
puzzling to himself he said, wondering to himself:
"Why are 'the stone things' of the boat smashed to pieces?
And why is someone not its master sailing on it?
The one who is coming is not a man of mine, . . .
I keep looking but not . . .
I keep looking but not . . .
I keep looking . . ."

[20 lines are missing here.]

207 Utanapishtim said to Gilgamesh:
"Why are your cheeks emaciated, your expression desolate?
Why is your heart so wretched, your features so haggard?
Why is there such sadness deep within you?
Why do you look like one who has been traveling a long distance
so that ice and heat have seared your face?
. . . you roam the wilderness?"

214 Gilgamesh spoke to Utanapishtim saying:
"Should not my cheeks be emaciated, my expression desolate?
Should my heart not be wretched, my features not haggard?
Should there not be sadness deep within me?
Should I not look like one who has been traveling a long distance,
and should ice and heat not have seared my face?
. . . should I not roam the wilderness?
My friend who chased wild asses in the mountain, the panther
of the wilderness,
Enkidu, my friend, who chased wild asses in the mountain, the
panther of the wilderness,
we joined together, and went up into the mountain.
We grappled with and killed the Bull of Heaven,
we destroyed Humbaba who dwelled in the Cedar Forest,
we slew lions in the mountain passes!

227 My friend, whom I love deeply, who went through every hard-
ship with me,

Enkidu, my friend, whom I love deeply, who went through
                    every hardship with me,
the fate of mankind has overtaken him.
Six days and seven nights I mourned over him
and would not allow him to be buried
until a maggot fell out of his nose.
I was terrified *by his appearance*(?),
I began to fear death, and so roam the wilderness.
The issue of my friend oppresses me,
so I have been roaming long trails through the wilderness.
The issue of Enkidu, my friend, oppresses me,
so I have been roaming long roads through the wilderness.
How can I stay silent, how can I be still?
My friend whom I love has turned to clay;
Enkidu, my friend whom I love, has turned to clay!
Am I not like him? Will I lie down never to get up again?"

243 Gilgamesh spoke to Utanapishtim, saying:
"That is why (?) I must go on, to see Utanapishtim whom they
                    call 'The Faraway.'⁶
I went circling through all the mountains,
I traversed treacherous mountains, and crossed all the seas—
that is why (?) sweet sleep has not mellowed my face,
through sleepless striving I am strained,
my muscles are filled with pain.
I had not yet reached the tavern-keeper's area before my
                    clothing gave out.
I killed bear, hyena, lion, panther, tiger, stag, red-stag, and
                    beasts of the wilderness;
I ate their meat and wrapped their skins around me.⁷

6. Apparently Gilgamesh has not yet realized that he is already talking with Utanapishtim, whom he expected to look very different from an ordinary human being. (See beginning of Tablet XI.) It is only after Utanapishtim's soliloquy on death that Gilgamesh realizes whom he is speaking to.

7. The following three lines are fragmentary, and what is preserved is still obscure. These lines may be related to the equally obscure two lines in the Old Babylonian version which follow "He put on their skins and ate their meat" (clearly an echo of the present line): "*In* the wells, Gilgamesh, that which has never been, . . . my wind will lead on the waters (?)."

The gate of grief must be bolted shut, *sealed* with pitch and
                                                    bitumen!
As for me, dancing . . .
For me unfortunate(?) it(?) will root out . . ."
256 Utanapishtim spoke to Gilgamesh, saying:[8]
"Why, Gilgamesh, do you . . . sadness?
You who *were created* (?) from the flesh of gods and mankind
who made . . . like your father and mother?
Have you ever . . . Gilgamesh . . . to the fool . . .
They placed a chair in the Assembly, . . .
But to the fool they gave beer dregs instead of butter,
bran and cheap flour which like . . .
Clothed with a loincloth (?) like . . .
And . . . in place of a sash,
because he does not have . . .
does not have words of counsel . . .
268   Take care about it, Gilgamesh,
. . . their master . . .
. . . Sin . . .
. . . eclipse of the moon . . .
The gods are sleepless . . .
They are troubled, restless(?) . . .
Long ago it has been established . . .
You trouble yourself . . .
. . . your help . . .
If Gilgamesh . . . the temple of the gods
. . . the temple of the holy gods,
. . . the gods . . .
. . .
. . . mankind,
they took . . . for his fate.
You have toiled without cease, and what have you got?

8. The following speech, only partly intelligible, may be derived from traditional
Mesopotamian wisdom literature. The gist of Utanapishtim's remarks in lines 260–67
may be that "the village idiot . . . wears wretched clothes and eats bad food, but no one
accords him merit for that—he is just a fool." (Interpretation of Foster, "Gilgamesh:
Sex, Love and the Ascent of Knowledge," p. 41.)

Through toil you wear yourself out,
you fill your body with grief,
your long lifetime you are bringing near (to a premature end)!
Mankind, whose offshoot is snapped off like a reed in a
canebreak,
the fine youth and lovely girl
. . . death.

290 No one can see death,
no one can see the face of death,
no one can hear the voice of death,
yet there is savage death that snaps off mankind.
For how long do we build a household?
For how long do we seal a document?
For how long do brothers share the inheritance?
For how long is there to be jealousy in the land(?)?

298 For how long has the river risen and brought the overflowing
waters,
so that dragonflies drift down the river?[9]
The face that could gaze upon the face of the Sun
has never existed ever.
How alike are the sleeping(?) and the dead.
The image of Death cannot be depicted.
(Yes, you are a) human being, a man (?)!

305 After Enlil had pronounced the blessing,[10]
the Anunnaki, the Great Gods, assembled.

9. This and the next five lines are much disputed, and open to sharply different inter-
pretation. W. G. Lambert, who edited the entire speech of Utanapishtim in "The Theol-
ogy of Death," in B. Alster, ed., *Death in Mesopotamia* (vol. 8 of *Mesopotamia*;
Copenhagen, 1980), p. 56, proposes:

X vi 22 = 299	So that dragonflies drift on the river,
23	Their faces staring into the face of the sun god?
24	Suddenly there is nothing.
25	The prisoner and the dead are alike,
26	Death itself cannot be depicted.
27 = 304	But Lullu—man—is incarcerated.

10. Finishing his soliloquy on life and death, Utanapishtim here reveals how death
came to be the fate of mankind, and implicitly how Utanapishtim himself was spared.
This is apparently the "secret of the gods" that Gilgamesh has been seeking. These last
five lines refer to the "Myth of Atrahasis" (Atrahasis = Utanapishtim), in which Enlil
grudgingly allows the pious Atrahasis who escaped the Flood to live for eternity, but

Mammetum, she who fashions destiny, determined destiny
with them.
They established Death and Life,
309 but they did not make known 'the days of death.'"[11]

Enlil and the other gods then establish death for all other humans as a necessary means
of population control. The Flood Story is retold at length in Tablet XI.

11. The "days of death" probably means the day on which an individual's death will
occur, although some interpret the line to mean "they did not fix a limit to death."

TABLET
XI

It is only now that Gilgamesh realizes that he has been talking to Utanapishtim all along—he seems to have been expecting an extraordinary being whose secret of immortality he could seize by force. Abashed and perplexed, Gilgamesh asks how it came about that Utanapishtim, only a human, attained eternal life. Utanapishtim then reveals the "secret of the gods": how the Flood came about, and how he (with his family and some animals) was spared by obeying the instructions of his god, Ea, and by making offerings in thanksgiving. The gods, who had suffered from the loss of regular food offerings by mankind, persuaded the chief god Enlil to allow the pious Utanapishtim and his wife to live forever in a far corner of the world, at the "Mouth of the Rivers." To see whether the gods might make an exception also in Gilgamesh's case, Utanapishtim tests his "immortality potential," his ability to do without sleep. When confronted with the evidence of his human frailty, his need for sleep, Gilgamesh despairs. Utanapishtim expels the ferryman from his post for having brought Gilgamesh, and assigns him to restore Gilgamesh to his royal role and accompany him back to Uruk. They start to sail off but Utanapishtim calls him back, yielding to his wife's compassionate insistence that Gilgamesh be given something to show for his efforts. So it is that Utanapishtim tells another "secret of the gods." A "plant of rejuvenation" will allow Gilgamesh to regain his lost youth, apparently to live life over with the advantage of his new wisdom. Gilgamesh finds the plant but, curiously, seems not to have faith in it or Utanapishtim. Rather than eating it on the spot, he decides to test the plant on an old man of Uruk first. The delay is his undoing, because a snake sneaks up and carries the plant off. Gilgamesh returns home older and empty-handed, for there are no second chances in real life, much less immortality. The story of Gilgamesh's quest then ends suddenly where it began, echoing the words of Tablet I (lines 17–22) in homage to his achievement—the wall of Uruk and the text of the Epic itself.

Tablet XI is essentially complete, known from eight to twelve copies, more than any other tablet. No Old Babylonian or Hittite fragments with the conversation with Utanapishtim have yet been found.

TABLET XI

The Story of the Flood[1]

1 Gilgamesh spoke to Utanapishtim, the Faraway:
   "I have been looking at you,
   but your appearance is not strange—you are like me!
   You yourself are not different—you are like me!
   My mind was resolved to fight with you,
   (*but instead?*) my arm lies useless over you.
   Tell me, how is it that you stand in the Assembly of the Gods,
                                    and have found life?"
   Utanapishtim spoke to Gilgamesh, saying:
   "I will reveal to you, Gilgamesh, a thing that is hidden,
   a secret of the gods I will tell you!

11 Shuruppak, a city that you surely know,
   situated on the banks of the Euphrates,
   that city was very old, and there were gods inside it.
   The hearts of the Great Gods moved them to inflict the Flood.
   Their Father Anu uttered the oath (of secrecy),
   Valiant Enlil was their Adviser,
   Ninurta was their Chamberlain,
   Ennugi was their Minister of Canals.
   Ea, the Clever Prince(?),[2] was under oath with them
   so he repeated their talk to the reed house:

21   'Reed house, reed house! Wall, wall!

1. The Flood Story told here is an adaptation or excerpt from (a version of) the flood
episode in the "Myth of Atrahasis." The retelling of the Flood Story is not essential to
the advancement of the Gilgamesh narrative (the "secret of the gods" was already ex-
plained in Tablet X), and had not been incorporated into the Old Babylonian version. A
short Flood Story exists in the Sumerian language, but it is believed to have been derived
from the Akkadian-language story, and does not, therefore, derive from a more ancient
Sumerian tradition. For a discussion of the literary relationships of the Mesopotamian
Flood stories, see Tigay, *Evolution*, pp. 214–40.
2. The word *niššiku*, translated "Clever Prince," is a word applied only to the god
Ea/Enki, and its meaning is not definitely known. It seems to have connotations of clev-
erness or craftiness, which are pertinent to Ea's behavior in the Flood Story.

Hear, O reed house! Understand, O wall!
O man of Shuruppak, son of Ubartutu:
Tear down the house and build a boat!
Abandon wealth and seek living beings!
Spurn possessions and keep alive living beings!
Make all living beings go up into the boat.
The boat which you are to build,
its dimensions must measure equal to each other:
its length must correspond to its width.
Roof it over like the Apsu.'

32   I understood and spoke to my lord, Ea:
'My lord, thus is the command which you have uttered
I will heed and will do it.
But what shall I answer the city, the populace, and the
                                    Elders?'
Ea spoke, commanding me, his servant:
'You, well then, this is what you must say to them:
    "It appears that Enlil is rejecting me
    so I cannot reside in your *city* (?),
    nor set foot on Enlil's earth.
    I will go down to the Apsu to live with my lord, Ea,
    and upon you he will rain down abundance,
    a profusion of fowl, myriad(?) fishes.
    He will bring to you a harvest of wealth,
    in the morning he will let loaves of bread shower down,
    and in the evening a rain of wheat!"'

47   Just as dawn began to glow
the land assembled *around me*—
the carpenter carried his hatchet,
the reed worker carried his (flattening) stone,
. . . the men . . .

. . .

The child carried the pitch,
the weak brought whatever else was needed.
On the fifth day I laid out her exterior.

It was a field in area,[3]
its walls were each 10 times 12 cubits in height,
the sides of its top were of equal length, 10 times 12 cubits each.

58 I laid out its (interior) structure and drew a picture of it (?).
I provided it with six decks,
thus dividing it into seven (levels).
The inside of it I divided into nine (compartments).
I drove plugs (to keep out) water in its middle part.
I saw to the punting poles and laid in what was necessary.
Three times 3,600 (units) of raw bitumen I poured into the
bitumen kiln,
three times 3,600 (units of) pitch . . . into it,
there were three times 3,600 porters of casks who carried (vege-
table) oil,
apart from the 3,600 (units of) oil which they consumed (?)
and two times 3,600 (units of) oil which the boatman stored
away.

69 I butchered oxen for *the meat*(?),
and day upon day I slaughtered sheep.
I gave the workmen(?) ale, beer, oil, and wine, as if it were
river water,
so they could make a party like the New Year's Festival.
. . . and I set my hand to the oiling(?).
The boat was finished by sunset.
The launching was very difficult.
They had to keep carrying a runway of poles front to back,
until two-thirds of it had gone into the water(?).
Whatever I had I loaded on it:
whatever silver I had I loaded on it,
whatever gold I had I loaded on it.
All the living beings that I had I loaded on it,

---

3. The boat as described is clearly a cube, not at all like ordinary Mesopotamian boats, and is probably a theological allusion to the dimensions of a ziggurat, the Mesopotamian stepped temple tower. The ziggurat was a massive solid structure with a square base and four to seven levels, the maximum height being the same as the length and width; it served as a monumental platform for a temple that stood on top.

I had all my kith and kin go up into the boat,
all the beasts and animals of the field and the craftsmen I
had go up.

84 Shamash had set a stated time:[4]
'In the morning I will let loaves of bread shower down,
and in the evening a rain of wheat!
Go inside the boat, seal the entry!'
That stated time had arrived.
In the morning he let loaves of bread shower down,
and in the evening a rain of wheat.
I watched the appearance of the weather—
the weather was frightful to behold!
I went into the boat and sealed the entry.
For the caulking of the boat, to Puzuramurri, the boatman,
I gave the palace together with its contents.

96 Just as dawn began to glow
there arose from the horizon a black cloud.
Adad rumbled inside of it,
before him went Shullat and Hanish,
heralds going over mountain and land.
Erragal pulled out the mooring poles,
forth went Ninurta and made the dikes overflow.
The Anunnaki lifted up the torches,
setting the land ablaze with their flare.
Stunned shock over Adad's deeds overtook the heavens,
and turned to blackness all that had been light.
The . . . land shattered like a . . . pot.

108 All day long the South Wind blew . . . ,
blowing fast, *submerging the* mountain *in water*,
overwhelming *the people* like an attack.
No one could see his fellow,
they could not recognize each other in the torrent.
The gods were frightened by the Flood,
and retreated, ascending to the heaven of Anu.

4. Earlier, in lines 36–47, Ea, not Shamash, had given the stated time.

The gods were cowering like dogs, crouching by the outer wall.
Ishtar shrieked like a woman in childbirth,
the sweet-voiced Mistress of the Gods wailed:
    'The olden days have alas turned to clay,
    because I said evil things in the Assembly of the Gods!
    How could I say evil things in the Assembly of the Gods,
    ordering a catastrophe to destroy my people?!
    No sooner have I given birth to my dear people
    than they fill the sea like so many fish!'
124   The gods—those of the Anunnaki—were weeping with her,
the gods humbly sat weeping, sobbing with grief(?),
their lips burning, parched with thirst.
Six days and seven nights
came the wind and flood, the storm flattening the land.
When the seventh day arrived, the storm was pounding,
the flood was a war—struggling with itself like a woman
                            writhing (in labor).
The sea calmed, fell still, the whirlwind (and) flood stopped up.
132   I looked around all day long—quiet had set in
and all the human beings had turned to clay!
The terrain was as flat as a roof.
I opened a vent and fresh air (daylight?) fell upon the side of
                            my nose.
I fell to my knees and sat weeping,
tears streaming down the side of my nose.
I looked around for coastlines in the expanse of the sea,
and at twelve leagues there emerged a region (of land).
On Mt. Nimush the boat lodged firm,
Mt. Nimush held the boat, allowing no sway.
One day and a second Mt. Nimush held the boat, allowing
                            no sway.
A third day, a fourth, Mt. Nimush held the boat, allowing
                            no sway.
A fifth day, a sixth, Mt. Nimush held the boat, allowing
                            no sway.

145 When a seventh day arrived
I sent forth a dove and released it.
The dove went off, but came back to me;
no perch was visible so it circled back to me.
I sent forth a swallow and released it.
The swallow went off, but came back to me;
no perch was visible so it circled back to me.
I sent forth a raven and released it.
The raven went off, and saw the waters slither back.
It eats, it scratches, it bobs, but does not circle back to me.
155 Then I sent out everything in all directions and sacrificed
(a sheep).
I offered incense in front of the mountain-ziggurat.
Seven and seven cult vessels I put in place,
and (into the fire) underneath (or: into their bowls) I poured
reeds, cedar, and myrtle.
The gods smelled the savor,
the gods smelled the sweet savor,
and collected like flies over a (sheep) sacrifice.
Just then Beletili arrived.
She lifted up the large flies (beads)⁵ which Anu had made for
his enjoyment(?):
'You gods, as surely as I shall not forget this lapis lazuli
around my neck,
may I be mindful of these days, and never forget them!
The gods may come to the incense offering,
but Enlil may not come to the incense offering,
because without considering he brought about the Flood
and consigned my people to annihilation.'
170 Just then Enlil arrived.
He saw the boat and became furious,
he was filled with rage at the Igigi gods:
'Where did a living being escape?

5. A necklace with carved lapis lazuli fly beads, representing the dead offspring of the mother goddess Beletili/Aruru.

No man was to survive the annihilation!'
Ninurta spoke to Valiant Enlil, saying:
  'Who else but Ea could devise such a thing?
  It is Ea who knows every machination!'

178   Ea spoke to Valiant Enlil, saying:
  'It is *you*, O Valiant One, who is the Sage of the Gods.
  How, how could *you* bring about a Flood without consideration?
  Charge the violation to the violator,
  charge the offense to the offender,
  but be compassionate lest (mankind) be cut off,
  be patient lest *they be killed.*
  Instead of your bringing on the Flood,
  would that a lion had appeared to diminish the people!
  Instead of your bringing on the Flood,
  would that a wolf had appeared to diminish the people!
  Instead of your bringing on the Flood,
  would that famine had occurred to slay the land!
  Instead of your bringing on the Flood,
  would that (Pestilent) Erra had appeared to ravage the land!
  It was not I who revealed the secret of the Great Gods,
  I (only) made a dream appear to Atrahasis, and (thus) he
                     heard the secret of the gods.
  Now then! The deliberation should be about him!'

196   Enlil went up inside the boat
and, grasping my hand, made me go up.
He had my wife go up and kneel by my side.
He touched our forehead and, standing between us, he
                     blessed us:
  'Previously Utanapishtim was a human being.
  But now let Utanapishtim and his wife become like us,
                     the gods!
  Let Utanapishtim reside far away, at the Mouth of the Rivers.'
They took us far away and settled us at the Mouth of the Rivers."

A Chance at Immortality

[The Story of the Flood ends. Utanapishtim now addresses Gilgamesh again.]

204   "Now then, who will convene the gods on your behalf,
       that you may find the life that you are seeking?
       Wait! You must not lie down for six days and seven nights."
As soon as he sat down (with his head) between his legs
sleep, like a fog, blew upon him.
Utanapishtim said to his wife:
       "Look there! The man, the youth who wanted (eternal) life!
       Sleep, like a fog, blew over him."
His wife said to Utanapishtim the Faraway:
       "Touch him, let the man awaken.
       Let him return safely by the way he came.
       Let him return to his land by the gate through which he left."
216 Utanapishtim said to his wife:
       "Mankind is deceptive, and will deceive you.
       Come, bake loaves for him and keep setting them by his head
       and draw on the wall each day that he lay down."
She baked his loaves and placed them by his head
and marked on the wall the day that he lay down.
The first loaf was dessicated,
the second stale, the third moist(?), the fourth turned white,
                                                   its . . . ,
the fifth sprouted gray (mold), the sixth is still fresh.
The seventh—suddenly he touched him and the man awoke.
226 Gilgamesh said to Utanapishtim:
       "The very moment sleep was pouring over me
       you touched me and alerted me!"
Utanapishtim spoke to Gilgamesh, saying:
       "*Look over here*, Gilgamesh, count your loaves!
       You should be aware of what is *marked on the wall*!
       Your first loaf is dessicated,
       the second stale, the third moist, your fourth turned white,
                                                   its . . .

the fifth sprouted gray (mold), the sixth is still fresh.
The seventh—at that instant you awoke!"
Gilgamesh said to Utanapishtim the Faraway:
"O woe! What shall I do, Utanapishtim, where shall I go?
The Snatcher has taken hold of my flesh,
in my bedroom Death dwells,
and wherever I set foot there too is Death!"

Home Empty-Handed

241 Utanapishtim said to Urshanabi, the ferryman:
"May the harbor reject you, may the ferry landing reject you!
May you who used to walk its shores be denied its shores!
The man in front of whom you walk, matted hair chains
his body,
animal skins have ruined his beautiful skin.
Take him away, Urshanabi, bring him to the washing place.
Let him wash his matted hair in water like *ellu*.
Let him cast away his animal skin and have the sea carry it off,
let his body be moistened with fine oil,
let the wrap around his head be made new,
let him wear royal robes worthy of him!
Until he goes off to his city,
until he sets off on his way,
let his royal robe not become spotted, let it be perfectly new!"
255 Urshanabi took him away and brought him to the washing place.
He washed his matted hair with water like *ellu*.
He cast off his animal skin and the sea carried it off.
He moistened his body with fine oil,
and made a new wrap for his head.
He put on a royal robe worthy of him.
Until he went away to his city,
until he set off on his way,
his royal robe remained unspotted, it was perfectly clean.
Gilgamesh and Urshanabi boarded the boat,
they cast off the *magillu*-boat, and sailed away.

A Second Chance at Life

266 The wife of Utanapishtim the Faraway said to him:
    "Gilgamesh came here exhausted and worn out.
    What can you give him so that he can return to his land (with
                      honor)?"
Then Gilgamesh raised a punting pole
and drew the boat to shore.
Utanapishtim spoke to Gilgamesh, saying:
    "Gilgamesh, you came here exhausted and worn out.
    What can I give you so you can return to your land?
    I will disclose to you a thing that is hidden, Gilgamesh,
    a . . . I will tell you.
    There is a plant . . . like a boxthorn,
    whose thorns will prick your hand like a rose.
    If your hands reach that plant *you will become a young
                  man again.*"

279 Hearing this, Gilgamesh opened a conduit(?) (to the Apsu)
and attached heavy stones to his feet.
They dragged him down, to the Apsu they pulled him.
He took the plant, though it pricked his hand,
and cut the heavy stones from his feet,
letting the *waves*(?) throw him onto its shores.
Gilgamesh spoke to Urshanabi, the ferryman, saying:
    "Urshanabi, this plant is a plant against decay(?)
    by which a man can attain his survival(?).
    I will bring it to Uruk-Haven,
    and have an old man eat the plant to test it.
    The plant's name is 'The Old Man Becomes a Young Man.'[6]
    Then I will eat it and return to the condition of my youth."
At twenty leagues they broke for some food,
at thirty leagues they stopped for the night.

294 Seeing a spring and how cool its waters were,

6. The same as the apparent meaning of the name "Gilgamesh."

Gilgamesh went down and was bathing in the water.
A snake smelled the fragrance of the plant,
silently came up and carried off the plant.
While going back it sloughed off its casing.[7]
At that point Gilgamesh sat down, weeping,
his tears streaming over the side of his nose.
    "*Counsel me*, O ferryman Urshanabi!
For whom have my arms labored, Urshanabi?
For whom has my heart's blood roiled?
I have not secured any good deed for myself,
but done a good deed for the 'lion of the ground'![8]
Now the high waters are coursing twenty leagues distant,[9]
as I was opening the conduit(?) I turned my equipment over
                    into it (?).
What can I find (to serve) as a marker(?) for me?
I will turn back (from the journey by sea) and leave the boat by
                    the shore!"

Deeds Over Death

310 At twenty leagues they broke for some food,
at thirty leagues they stopped for the night.
They arrived in Uruk-Haven.
Gilgamesh said to Urshanabi, the ferryman:
    "Go up, Urshanabi, onto the wall of Uruk and walk around.
Examine its foundation, inspect its brickwork thoroughly—
is not (even the core of) the brick structure of kiln-fired brick,
and did not the Seven Sages themselves lay out its plan?

---

7. This scene is an etiological story of how the snake came to shed its old skin—after eating a "plant of rejuvenation."

8. "Lion of the ground" is a very rare phrase occurring only here and in scribal word lists. A translation "chameleon" has been proposed because the "chameleon" in Greek appeared to be composed of the same elements, "lion of the ground." "Chameleon" is now believed, however, to be not a native Greek compound, but itself a loan translation from Semitic.

9. This line and those following are fragmentary, and the sense is not at all certain. The verbal tenses in line 309 are normally understood as "Would that I had turned back and left the boat by the shore." A past conditional could reflect Gilgamesh's regret at

One league city, one league palm gardens, one league lowlands,
the open area(?) of the Ishtar Temple,
319   three leagues and the open area(?) of Uruk it (the wall)
encloses."

---

his failed journey. On the other hand, the adjacent lines suggest that Gilgamesh and Urshanabi now abandon the sea voyage for lack of certain equipment (l. 307) and continue overland to Uruk. The present translation reflects this understanding.

Appendixes

APPENDIX A

Glossary

This glossary lists the deities, persons, and places mentioned in the Epic. The name given in parentheses is the equivalent Sumerian deity.

Adad. The chief Storm God.

Aja. The wife of the Sun God, Shamash.

Anu. The original Sky God, the most ancient deity of Sumer, called the Father of the Gods. His sacred city was Uruk, on the Euphrates River. His Temple was the Eanna, "House of Anu," which was from an early period also the temple of his daughter, Inanna (Sumerian) or Ishtar (Akkadian).

Anunnaki. The Anunnaki were a group of 50 gods, sons of Anu; the "Seven Great Anunnaki" were the seven gods who "fixed the destinies" and the only ones who could authorize change in the constitution of the universe.

Anzu. A mythological lion-headed eagle. Often shown frontally with wings outstretched.

Apsu. The freshwater sea flowing under the earth, the domain of the god Ea (Enki). Water containers, called *apsu*, were used in temple rituals.

Aruru. The Mother Goddess, who created mankind in the "Myth of Atrahasis," where she was called Beletili, "Lady of the Gods."

Ashnan. The Goddess of Grain.

Atrahasis. An epithet applied to the survivor of the Flood, and also used as his name. The epithet means "exceedingly attentive," or "exceedingly wise." He is the same as Utanapishtim in Tablet XI.

Beletili. See *Aruru.*

Beletseri. The female scribe of the Netherworld. The name means "Lady of the Wilderness," wilderness being a synonym for Netherworld.

Bibbu. A planet or possibly a comet.

Cedar Forest. The locale of the Cedar Forest in the original Sumerian short epic was probably east of the Zagros Mountains in ancient Elam (southwestern Iran), the source of timber in that period. In the Old Babylonian version, however, the Cedar Forest is clearly located in the northwest, probably in the Amanus Mountains of southern Turkey, which had become the new source of cedar by the time of the Old Babylonian author. The identification of the tree as "cedar" is traditional but not certain—it may have been a pine.

Ea. (Enki). The god of the subterranean freshwater sea, the Apsu, whose cult center was in Eridu, in far southern Mesopotamia. In myth he is often presented as a trickster, using clever stratagems and verbal games to achieve his ends without technically violating the "rules."

Eanna. The Temple of Anu and Inanna/Ishtar in Uruk. The name means "House of Anu."

Egalmah. The temple of Ninsun in Uruk. The name means "Exalted Palace."

Enkidu. In the Akkadian Gilgamesh Epic Enkidu was a primitive man living among wild animals until seduced and domesticated by a harlot. He became the cherished friend of King Gilgamesh. In the Sumerian epic tales about Gilgamesh he was merely the servant and companion of Gilgamesh. Enkidu, upon his creation by the mother goddess, is called "born of the Silence [= the Still of Night], endowed with strength by Ninurta" (I, 85).

Enlil. The chief deity of the Sumerian pantheon, whose name means "Lord Wind," he was ultimately in charge of determining destinies. His cult center was in Nippur, on the Euphrates River. His temple was the Ekur, the "Mountain House." His wife was Ninlil.

Ennugi. There were several minor gods or demons of this name; one was called Chief Canal Minister of the gods, another a doorkeeper of Ereshkigal.

Ereshkigal. The "Queen of the Netherworld," whose husband was Nergal.

Erra. The much-feared God of Pestilence, subject of a major myth composed in the first millennium B.C., the "Erra Epic."

Erragal. Another name for Nergal.

Etana. The king of the city Kish after the Flood. The inclusion of Etana in Enkidu's premonition of the Netherworld must be because of some particular relevance of Etana's fate to Enkidu's situation. The fragments of the "Myth of Etana" tell that Ishtar selected the young Etana to be king, and that he sought the magical "plant of birth" for his barren wife. An eagle helped him by carrying him up to the heavens, but then fell back to earth. The last traces speak of another meeting with a seemingly angry Ishtar, and there is somewhat later a reference to Etana's ghost.

Euphrates. The western of the two major rivers of Mesopotamia, along which ancient settlements clustered. It originates in the mountains of Turkey, and then flows through Syria down the western part of Iraq. It was navigable along most of its length, and was the basis of agriculture, providing fertile silt and water in its annual overflow.

Hanish. A minor weather god, usually paired with Shullat, the two being heralds of the Storm God, Adad.

Hermon. The highest peak of the Anti-Lebanon Mountains.

Humbaba. A protective demon, the Guardian of the Cedar Forest, appointed by the god Enlil to protect the sacred Cedar(s). The cultural origin of Humbaba is Elamite (ancient southwestern Iran), "Humbaba" being a form of the name of the chief god of the Elamite pantheon, Humpan. He was endowed with extraordinary power to detect trespassers and a terror-inspiring appearance to drive them away. "Humbaba's roar is a Flood, his mouth is Fire, his breath is Death . . . he can hear any rustling in his forest from 60 leagues away!" What Gilgamesh actually sees when he meets Humbaba is lost in a break, but the traces seem to indicate that Humbaba did not turn out to be the monstrous ogre Gilgamesh was expecting. Humbaba's long, strange dialogues indicate that he had known Gilgamesh and Enkidu previously. The character of Humbaba and his attributes differ considerably from those of the Sumerian version(s) of this episode and from the Old Babylonian version.

Igigi. A group of gods who were subject to the Anunnaki and did manual labor for them.

Irkalla. Another name of the Netherworld.

Irnini. Another name of Ishtar, in her ferocious aspect.

Ishara. A name of Ishtar in her cultic role during the Sacred Marriage rite.

Ishtar (Inanna). The Goddess of Love and War, daughter of Anu, lover of Tammuz, who shared the Eanna Temple in Uruk with Anu. Ishtar's most prominent role was that of the voluptuous Goddess of Love, and women votaries of her cult had some sexual duties. The harlot Shamhat was probably one of Ishtar's votaries.

Ishullanu. A date gardener, the last of Ishtar's six lovers in the litany of ruined men in Tablet VI. This section may allude to the Sumerian myth involving Inanna and the gardener Shukalletuda.

Lebanon. The coastal mountain range running the length of Lebanon.

Lugalbanda. One of the kings of Uruk after the Flood; the name means "Young King." In Sumerian literature he is the husband of Ninsun and father of Gilgamesh.

Lullubu. The wild mountain people of western Iran.

Mammetum. Another name of the Mother Goddess, Aruru.

Mashu. The two mountains through which the sun rises.

Mouth of the Rivers. "Mouth of the Rivers" is attested in early second millennium non-literary documents as an actual geographical name, and was probably located where the Tigris and Euphrates rivers flow into the Persian Gulf.

Nergal. The husband of Ereshkigal, and with her ruler of the Netherworld.

Nimush. The name of the mountain where the boat landed after the Flood. The cuneiform signs of the name have been traditionally read as Nisir, but recent scholarship indicates that Nimush is the more likely reading. The mountain is possibly to be identified with the peak Pir Omar Gudrun (9,000 ft.) in the mountains of eastern Iraq.

Ninsun. The divine mother of Gilgamesh, wife of Lugalbanda. Her name means "Lady, Wild Cow." In the epic her name is sometimes written as a personal name without a divine determinative, and composed of the epithet *rimat* ("wild cow" in Akkadian) and Ninsun. The motif of the "good cow" who gives birth to kings is well documented in Sumerian literature.

Ninurta. God of War. Ninurta may have some connection with the land of Elam (ancient southwestern Iran). A list of gods identifies the god of Elam, Inshushinak, as "Ninurta of the Silence."

Nippur. The religious capital, the cult center of Enlil, located in the center of Mesopotamia.

Nisaba. The Goddess of Grain, depicted with waving sheaves of grain for hair.

Puzuramurri. The boatman who caulked the boat for Utanapishtim, receiving the palace as gift or payment. This is a good Old Babylonian personal name, but no historical referent can be identified.

Rimat-Ninsun. See Ninsun.

Seven Sages. According to various traditions, the Sages or Master Craftsmen lived before the Flood and taught mankind all crafts and civilization.

Shamash. The Sun God, who was god of justice and who hated "evil," "demons," and secret, hidden behavior such as witchcraft. The role of the Sun God is markedly different in the versions of the Epic. Understanding the political-religious significance of the change in his role must await the promised publication of the Sumerian epics.

Shamhat. The name of the harlot (*harimtu*) who introduces Enkidu to human living, estranging him from the world of nature. Shamhat is attested as a female personal name in Old Babylonian documents. Shamhat in the Epic is probably one of the harlots in the service of the Ishtar Temple. (The common translation "prostitute" is avoided here because its modern meaning—illicit sex for private gain—is inappropriate in the context of the Mesopotamian temple.)

Shullat. A minor weather deity, usually paired with Hanish, the two being heralds of the Storm God, Adad.

Shuruppak. One of the most ancient cities of Sumer. It is located about 30 km north of Uruk; the modern name of the site is Fara.

Siduri. The tavern-keeper (sometimes translated "beer maid") who directs Gilgamesh to the ferryman who will take him to Utanapishtim. Essentially an empty character in the Standard Version, in the Old Babylonian she delivers a short speech on human fulfillment.

Silili. The name of the mother of a stallion, possibly from an unknown folktale.

Sin. The Moon God, chief deity of Ur.

Sippar. City of northern Babylonia whose chief deity was the Sun God, Shamash.

Sumukan. The God of Wild Animals, symbolized in particular by his shaggy skin.

Tammuz (Dumuzi). In the context of Tablet VI, Tammuz is the lover and husband of Ishtar. He is a nature god, the god of vegetation that grows, dies, and then rises from the earth again each year. Lamentations for the dying god were a central feature of his cult.

Ubartutu. The king of Shuruppak and father of Utanapishtim.

Ulaja. The Karun River of southwestern Iran, flowing south and west of Susa, between Sumer and Elam. Its occurrence in the Epic supports other evidence that in the original Sumerian epics the Gilgamesh adventures were associated with Elam or other points east.

Urshanabi. The ferryman across the river of the Netherworld, which separates the world of the living from the dead. Urshanabi (Sursunabu in the Old Babylonian) is not a normal Sumerian personal name but means "Servant of Two-Thirds," a clear reference to his role (at the end of the Epic) as servant to Gilgamesh, who was two-thirds god.

Uruk. A city of ancient Sumer, located on the Euphrates River in southern Mesopotamia. One of the oldest and most sacred cities of Sumerian history, Uruk was the seat of the second dynasty to rule Sumer after the Flood. The site (modern name: Warka) was first excavated by the German Archaeological Institute in 1913. Among their finds was a city wall about five and one-half miles in circumference, dating to the Early Dynastic period, the probable time of the historical Gilgamesh. The description of Uruk as consisting of equal areas of habitation (= "city"), date gardens, and lowlands appears only in the Standard Version, and is therefore a late addition of no relevance for the Uruk of the historical Gilgamesh in the Early Dynastic period.

Utanapishtim (Ziusudra). The man (a king) who was allowed to survive the Flood, and was then given eternal life in a remote corner of the world. The name is not a normal personal name but an epithet meaning (approximately) "he has found life." In the "Myth of Atrahasis" from which the Flood Story in the Epic was excerpted, the survivor of the Flood is called Atrahasis, "exceedingly wise." He was the son of Ubartutu, the king of Shuruppak, a city of Sumer northwest of Uruk.

APPENDIX B

Tablet XII

In the Standard Version the Epic of Gilgamesh consisted of twelve tablets. Why, then, have I presented only eleven in this translation? The decision to eliminate Tablet XII was a matter of personal judgment, shared by many others, that though Tablet XII may be literally a part of the Epic (the subscript of Tablet XI indicates it has a sequel, and the subscript on Tablet XII identifies it as "Tablet XII" of the Gilgamesh series), it is not part of it in literary terms.

Tablet XII begins abruptly, with Gilgamesh lamenting the loss of two objects that had fallen into the Netherworld. When Enkidu, his servant, volunteers to retrieve them, Gilgamesh cautions him strictly about how to behave lest he be "seized" by the Netherworld and not allowed to return. Enkidu then does everything he was instructed not to do, and the Netherworld seizes him. Gilgamesh pleads with the god Enlil in Nippur, then with Sin in Ur, but they give him no satisfaction. In Eridu the god Ea, the god of the subterranean sea, does afford some limited help by opening a hole in the earth that allows the ghost of Enkidu to come forth. After the friends embrace, Gilgamesh asks what happens in the Netherworld; when Enkidu tells him of the wormy decay of the body, Gilgamesh in despair sits in the dust. Gilgamesh then asks Enkidu what has become of various persons in the Netherworld. The litany of fates follows this form: "Did you see him who had one son?" "I saw." "How does he fare?" "He weeps bitterly at the nail which was driven into his wall." The one who had seven sons sits as a companion of the gods and listens to music. The one who has no one to care for him eats scraps of leftovers thrown away in the streets. The text ends as abruptly as it began.

This tablet is clearly inconsistent with the previous eleven-tablet epic in several ways. First, Enkidu is still alive at the beginning of Tablet XII, though he had already died in Tablet VII. The tablet is also stylistically at odds with the rest of the Epic because it is almost a literal translation of half of a Sumerian-language myth called "Gilgamesh, Enkidu, and the Netherworld." Though many of the episodes of the Akkadian-language Epic were based on Sumerian prototypes, they were profoundly modified and adapted to the new author's purpose. Tablet XII bears few marks of such creative adaptation, and lacks any attempt at logical transition from Tablet XI. Indeed, it breaks the formal completeness of the Epic, which had come full circle between the survey of Uruk in Tablet I (lines 17–22) and the same survey at the end of Tablet XI (lines 302–7). Furthermore, the only part that bears any relation to the central concern of the main Epic (death) is Enkidu's litany of fates, occupying only the last half of Tablet XII. The first half of the tablet is essentially irrelevant and makes sense only in the context of the Sumerian myth from which it was excerpted. One wonders whether this lengthy buildup to Enkidu's report was included primarily to provide some bulk to the text, which is still only 175 lines long. Many scholars hold, in short, that Tablet XII is an "inorganic appendage to the eleven tablets which constituted the original form of the late version." (See Tigay, *Evolution*, p. 27.)

On the other hand, since it *was* appended there must have been some rationale for it, whatever our opinion of its literary quality and relevance. Scholarly speculation on Tablet XII identifies many possible reasons, but the most likely, in my opinion, is that it connects the Gilgamesh of the Epic to the Gilgamesh of institutional Mesopotamian religion, where he was known as king of the Netherworld. This tablet explains how knowledge of the conditions in the Netherworld came to be imparted to Gilgamesh. (See Tigay, *Evolution*, pp. 106–7.)

Tablet XII together with its Sumerian source is an extremely interesting document of mythology and anthropology, revealing the cultural evaluations of various social conditions by showing the fate of people embodying them in the Netherworld. As literature, however, it seems the work of a pedestrian spirit, perhaps of a prominent scribe trying to integrate all Gilgamesh traditions merely for the sake of scholarly comprehensiveness. In any event, the attempt was not well executed, and I prefer to rest with the eleven-tablet Epic.

APPENDIX C

Mesopotamian Languages and Writing

LANGUAGES AND LOCATIONS

Sumerian is the language of the early inhabitants of southern Mesopotamia. Despite diligent efforts, it still cannot be related to any other known language. Sumerian gradually died out as the vernacular, probably by 2000 B.C., although it was retained for royal inscriptions, religious writing, and literature. The geographical area Sumer is the far southern part of modern-day Iraq.*

Akkadian is a Semitic language, of the east Semitic group, introduced into Mesopotamia in the middle of the third millennium B.C. The oldest dialect, called "Old Akkadian," was written ca. 2400–2000 B.C. Thereafter scholars distinguish two main regional dialects, Babylonian and Assyrian. Babylonia is in the south, from the confluence of the Tigris and Euphrates near Baghdad to the Persian Gulf, and the name derives from Babylon, the capital city of the kings ruling that area. Assyria is the area north of the confluence of the Tigris and Euphrates rivers, chiefly along the Tigris as far as the mountains of southern Turkey, and the name derives from Assur, the capital city. The Babylonian and Assyrian dialects are further subdivided into chronological periods called Old, Middle, and Neo, which coincide by and large with political periods of the same names.

There is a last dialect that has no specific reference to chronology or geography. Standard Babylonian is a literary dialect which developed out of Old Babylonian sometime between the sixteenth and twelfth centuries. It was used by all scribes for writing literature, regardless of whether they lived in Assyria or Babylonia. Hence the modern designation "standard."

CUNEIFORM WRITING

The word "cuneiform" comes from the Latin *cuneus* ("wedge, angle") and means writing with "wedge-shaped" strokes. Cuneiform script consists of "signs" of from one to ten strokes, formed by impressing the end of a reed stylus into clay, producing a line with a wedge-like head. (In the earliest stages

---

* Sumer (not Sumeria) is the term for southern Babylonia, the area inhabited by the Sumerians. There is no city called "Sumer," and the form "Sumeria" found in some popular writing is based on a false analogy with the forms Babylonia, Assyria, and Mesopotamia.

the signs were pictographic, with curved lines, rather than linear and wedged. This is called "pictographic cuneiform.") *

The script was developed in Sumer, southern Mesopotamia, in about 3000 B.C. out of the earlier "numerical notation" system using clay tokens impressed in clay. It was first used for the monosyllabic Sumerian language, with each sign representing a word (logogram). By the late third millennium it was adapted to write an unrelated language of Mesopotamia, called Akkadian. To represent Akkadian, a polysyllabic language, the script developed into a syllabary, with each sign representing simply a sound, and a series of signs "spelling" a word. The appearance of the signs changed enormously over the 3,000 years of cuneiform, the original pictograms becoming increasingly linear and conventional until one can perceive no relationship between the late forms of a sign and the original object.†

Cuneiform and Akkadian were gradually supplanted by the Aramaic language, written in alphabetic script with ink on parchment. Cuneiform became restricted to ever smaller scholarly circles, and more esoteric, scientific writing. Cuneiform was still used by a handful of scholars of Babylon as late as the first century A.D.,‡ though by then it had been reduced to only essential elements of astronomical notation.

---

* This is not the place to discuss the very complex issue of the nature and development of cuneiform writing. The interested reader is fortunate to have a recent short monograph on the subject available by a noted expert from the British Museum: C. B. Walker, *Cuneiform: Reading the Past* (Berkeley, Calif., 1987).

† The standard "book of sign forms" for Assyriologists is René Labat, *Manuel d'épigraphie accadienne* (revised and corrected by F. Malbran-Labat; Paris, 1976).

‡ The last cuneiform tablet containing a date belongs to the first century A.D., but there are also a few tablets that may be dated on paleographic grounds (the shape of the signs or letters) to the second or even third century A.D.

APPENDIX D

For Further Reading

I list below selected books and articles on the Epic of Gilgamesh and several general works on Mesopotamian culture.

THE EPIC OF GILGAMESH

An older English translation by Assyriologists is E. A. Speiser and A. Kirk Grayson, "The Epic of Gilgamesh," in the large collection of ancient texts edited by James B. Pritchard: *Ancient Near Eastern Texts Relating to the Old Testament* (Princeton, N.J.: Princeton Univ. Press, 3d edition with supplement, 1969). The paperback version is *The Ancient Near East. Vol. 1: An Anthology of Texts and Pictures* (1958); *Vol. 2: A New Anthology of Texts and Pictures* (1975).

"Translations" derived from other translations include John Gardner and John Maier, *Gilgamesh* (New York: Knopf, 1984; paperback, Random House, 1985); and N. K. Sandars, *The Epic of Gilgamesh* (New York: Penguin, 1960; 2d rev. ed. 1972).

The Epic, or Mesopotamian literature, has also inspired a number of popularizations and works of fiction: Robert Silverberg, *Gilgamesh the King* (New York: Arbor House, 1984); John C. Gardner, *The Sunlight Dialogues* (New York: Ballantine, 1982; Random House, 1987); Elizabeth Jamison Hodges, *A Song for Gilgamesh* (New York: Atheneum, 1971); Jennifer Westwood, *Gilgamesh & Other Babylonian Tales* (New York: Coward-McCann, 1970); D. G. Bridson, *The Quest for Gilgamesh* (Cambridge, Eng.: Rampant Lions Press, 1972); Herbert Mason, *Gilgamesh: A Verse Narrative* (New York: Mentor, 1972). The reader might also find the following two articles of interest: John R. Maier, "Charles Olson and the Poetic Uses of Mesopotamian Scholarship," *Journal of the American Oriental Society*, vol. 103 (1983), pp. 223–27; Jack M. Sasson, "On Musical Settings for Cuneiform Literature: A Discography," *Journal of the American Oriental Society*, vol. 103 (1983), pp. 233–35. These are modern compositions; the ancient Epic was not, as far as is known, associated with musical performance.

MESOPOTAMIAN CULTURE AND HISTORY

For very readable and informative descriptions of Mesopotamian society, culture, and daily life, with a minimum of political history, see H. W. F. Saggs, *The Greatness That Was Babylon* (New York: New American Library, 1962), and *The Might That Was Assyria* (London: Sidgwick & Jackson, 1984). The last chapter of the latter, "The Rediscovery of Assyria," describes the famous first archaeologists in Assyria and the modern international expeditions. The author's enthusiasm for his subject makes even the political history engaging.

For the nature and development of cuneiform writing, see C. B. Walker, *Cuneiform: Reading the Past* (Berkeley: Univ. of Calif. Press, 1987).

LITERATURE

The most comprehensive and up-to-date survey in English of Akkadian literature is Erica Reiner, *Your Thwarts in Pieces, Your Mooring Rope Cut. Poetry from Babylonia and Assyria*, Michigan Studies in the Humanities, vol. 5 (Ann Arbor: Michigan Slavic Publications, 1985). A. Leo Oppenheim's *Ancient Mesopotamia. Portrait of a Dead Civilization* (Chicago: Univ. of Chicago Press, 2d ed. 1977) is interpretive rather than descriptive, and requires some background in Mesopotamian studies to understand fully. Translations of some Sumerian literature can be found in Samuel Noah Kramer, *From the Poetry of Sumer. Creation, Glorification, Adoration* (Berkeley: Univ. of California Press, 1979), and Thorkild Jacobsen, *The Harps that Once . . .* (New Haven, Conn.: Yale Univ. Press, 1987).

A catalogue of all identifiable literary texts—many fragmentary and unknown outside of scholarly circles—is given in the article "Literatur" in *RealLexikon der Assyriologie*, vol. 7 (1987): Sumerian, by Dietz O. Edzard, pp. 35–48, and Akkadian, by W. Röllig, pp. 48–66.

ART

Figures shown in art are seldom identified by inscription and hence their identification is a matter of interpretation. While some older books were rather liberal in seeing heroes of mythology and epic, especially Gilgamesh and Enkidu, in art, advances in research often prove other identifications, as comparison of subsequent editions of art books reveals. The most recent surveys of Mesopotamian art are in German. André Parrot, *Sumer und Akkad*, Universum der Kunst vol. 1 (Munich, 4th ed., 1983), and *Assur. Mesopotamische Kunst vom XIII. vorchristlichen Jahrhundert bis zum*

Tode Alexanders des Grossen, Universum der Kunst vol. 2 (Munich, 3d ed. in preparation), are revised editions of his original French works. The English versions available are *Sumer: The Dawn of Art* and *The Arts of Assyria* (Golden Press, New York, 1961). Anton Moortgat, *Die Kunst des alten Mesopotamien. Vol. 1: Sumer und Akkad* and *Vol. 2: Babylon und Assur* (Cologne: DuMonte Dokumente, 1982 and 1984), are the revised and expanded versions of his single-volume work published in 1967.